Merry Elf-ing Christmas

BETH BOLDEN

Copyright © 2021 Beth Bolden.

All rights reserved. No part of this publication may be reproduced, distributed or transmitted in any form or by any means, including photocopying, recording, or other electronic or mechanical methods, without the prior written permission of the publisher, except in the case of brief quotations embodied in critical reviews and certain other noncommercial uses permitted by copyright law. For permission requests, write to the publisher, at the address below.

Beth Bolden Books

www.bethbolden.com

beth@bethbolden.com

Publisher's Note: This is a work of fiction. Names, characters, places, and incidents are a product of the author's imagination. Locales and public names are sometimes used for atmospheric purposes. Any resemblance to actual people, living or dead, or to businesses, companies, events, institutions, or locales is completely coincidental.

Book Layout © 2021 Beth Bolden

Book Cover © 2021 Sleepy Fox Studio

The people in the images are models and should not be connected to the characters in the book. Any resemblance is incidental.

Ordering Information:

Quantity sales. Special discounts are available on quantity purchases by corporations, associations, and others. For details, contact Beth Bolden at the address above.

Merry Elf-ing Christmas/ Beth Bolden. -- 1st ed.

Contents

1. Chapter One	1
2. Chapter Two	19
3. Chapter Three	41
4. Chapter Four	63
5. Chapter Five	79
6. Chapter Six	93
7. Chapter Seven	111
8. Chapter Eight	125
9. Chapter Nine	147
10. Chapter Ten	165
11. Chapter Eleven	177
Epilogue	197
Beth's Books	203
About Beth	209
Acknowledgments	211

Chapter One

Aidan was supposed to be in Ireland.

He was supposed to be counting golden coins, buffing cauldrons and helping his boss, the vice president of Leprechaun Operations, triangulate where the end of the next rainbow would land.

Instead, he was in Santa's sleigh.

Currently freezing his balls off.

His friend Ronan had said that "weirder things had happened," but Aidan wasn't sure that there was much weirder than at the young age of sixty-seven discovering that he wasn't meant to be at Tír na nÓg, but instead that he'd apparently been born under a unique northern star, under a particular set of circumstances—the same circumstances that a North Pole elf had once foretold would produce the Elf Who Would Save Christmas.

AKA the Christmas Savior.

Aidan was flattered, but the truth was, he didn't want to save Christmas.

He wanted to find the end of the next rainbow.

Santa—no, Aidan reminded himself, *Sam*, as he'd introduced himself a few weeks back, with twinkling blue eyes and a

1

welcoming smile—turned to him. "Want to stop for a snack?" he asked.

Aidan actually didn't. He wanted to finish this interminable night and get off this sleigh and stop shivering, *finally*.

The magic of Christmas *blah blah blah* had lasted just about as long as it took for that first blast of arctic air to sneak up the back of his fur-lined cloak.

"Sure, we could get a snack," Aidan said instead, because he was supposed to be assisting, and as Edmund, head of the North Pole elves, had told him when he'd pulled him aside for one last hissed, hurried set of instructions, that meant Santa got whatever he wanted.

"This night," Edmund said in that annoyingly stentorian voice of his, "is for Santa. It's Santa's night."

"Sam," Aidan had responded impudently, earning him one of Edmund's trademark frosty glares. "He told me to call him Sam."

Edmund had sniffed, clearly unamused. "If that is what Santa said, then so be it."

He'd learned that much during his last six weeks in the North Pole; Santa's word was freaking *law*.

Even the leprechauns hadn't wielded quite so much power.

But then with Sam, it wasn't really power. He ruled with good old-fashioned love, inspiring an adoring crowd who would gladly trample anyone who didn't feel the same.

The good news was that up til now, Aidan had managed to keep his apathy under wraps.

If Edmund or any of the other North Pole elves ever found out about it, he was screwed.

Sam pulled the sleigh, powered by its flying doohicky—Edmund had forwarded him the complicated plans that he'd glanced over and understood exactly *zero* of—down through the clouds of Chicago, snow thick on the ground.

Somehow, eventually he'd have to actually be able to take the sleigh apart and put it back together, or so Edmund had told him, but he'd been given a pass since it was just his first year. Aidan wasn't particularly looking forward to it.

Invisibility was one of the elves' greatest strengths, and their camouflaging magic helped keep the sleigh under wraps. It was the one thing the North Pole and the Tír na nÓg elves had in common: they were really good at making things disappear.

Still, you had to be careful, as Edmund had lectured Aidan about a dozen times. The sleigh might be invisible, but if they landed in a snowbank, the tracks would show. And if anyone ever bumped into it, the invisibility would fade, abruptly, exposing their secrets to humans.

AKA The Worst Thing Ever.

Sam jerked the reins, crisscrossing the sleigh through a forest of skyscrapers, and finally landing them in a dank, smelly alley.

Yay Christmas! Aidan thought weakly.

He missed the endless, sweet-smelling fields of Ireland.

He couldn't even remember the last time he'd seen *grass*. It was all buried, if it had ever existed at all, under all the snow at the North Pole.

Belinda had said he'd get used to it.

Aidan wasn't sure that was true, but unless he miraculously figured out that he'd actually been born under a different star, nothing was going to change anytime soon.

"Here we are," Sam said, patting him firmly on the back. "You know what I like."

Aidan barely resisted rolling his eyes as he climbed down from the sleigh. He pulled his hood up, hopefully hiding his telltale ears—the only sign he wasn't human, other than his slightly shorter height—and started to pick his way through the unpleasant-smelling snowdrifts in the alley.

"Just watch out for yellow snow," Ronan had said, hugging him one last time before he'd left Tír na nÓg, and sadly seeing the noxious snowdrifts now, spotted with dirt and God knew what else, Aidan wasn't sure he'd been wrong.

When Aidan reached the entrance to the alley, he turned left, pretty sure that when Sam had swung the sleigh around this way to get to the alley, he'd spotted the bright lights of a convenience store, still open despite the late hour and the fact it was Christmas Eve.

He'd never been in an American convenience store, but one thing Tír na nÓg had never been short on was technology and as many American TV shows and movies as he and Ronan could get their hands on, so as he pushed the door in, he wasn't particularly surprised by the harsh lighting or the shelves and shelves of cheap junk food.

There was a man sitting at the front counter, and even under the bright fluorescent lights, Aidan stopped dead in his tracks, not just merely astonished, but *shocked*.

The guy was attractive.

Not just attractive.

He was breath-stuttering-in-Aidan's-lungs, pulse-accelerating, palms-sweating hot.

His slightly too long dark hair swooped over his forehead in a beguiling curl, equally dark eyes piercing Aidan with their intelligent intensity, and the jaw, under a layer of scruff, could've cut glass.

"Hey," the guy said, and Aidan only had a split second to prepare himself for the smile that blasted through him.

It wasn't enough. He felt the power of that smile, the inherent charm of it, in every muscle, in every bone, in every pathetic organ of his body.

Aidan had met attractive men before. He'd lived in *Ireland* for God's sake, and even though the magic of the accent had been completely lost on him, there'd been plenty of good-looking guys there.

He'd even slept with a few of them, on the nights that he and Ronan had snuck out of the compound.

But he'd never had his heart and his cock get on the exact same page before, and scream, *yes, this is exactly what you want. Over him. Under him. Talking to him all night long, until you've shared all your secrets and you've heard all of his.*

The man's smile morphed from friendly and open to something resembling concern.

Aidan didn't know why it had changed so abruptly. Wished it would change back.

Then realized he was still standing halfway to the potato chip aisle, jaw dropped, and he hadn't uttered a single sound except maybe a hungry whimper.

He hadn't even said hi back.

"Uh, hello," Aidan said. Not his greatest work, but he wasn't supposed to be here to be flirting with a hot stranger. He was supposed to be grabbing . . . *something* for Sam.

What did Sam like again?

The smile was back, crinkling right at the edges of his mouth, and Aidan was mesmerized again. "Looking for something to snack on?" he asked.

"My boss is," Aidan said. He'd nearly said *Sam*, or even worse *Santa*, and that would have been difficult to explain.

The guy's eyebrows rose. "You're working on Christmas?"

Aidan crossed his arms over his chest, shooting him a look. "I'm not the only one," he said pointedly.

5

The smiling was bad enough; the laugh he let out, full and happy and carefree, it blew through Aidan's foundations, leaving him unmoored.

Ronan had always told him that one day he'd meet some guy he'd be irresistibly drawn to, that he wouldn't be able to help himself, and he'd fall hard and fast.

He hadn't *fallen,* because you couldn't fall for someone—even a really hot guy who worked at a convenience store—after exchanging less than twenty-five words.

Still, Aidan kind of hated Ronan right now, for being so insufferably right.

"It's not really working if you're the first customer I've had in hours," the guy said conversationally. There was still that flirtatious glint to his eyes.

Aidan didn't want to look away, even though Sam was waiting for him. The time was less of an issue, as one of the proprietary magics that the North Pole elves possessed was the ability to stop time.

It was the only way for Sam to make it around the world and deliver gifts to every child.

But if he didn't get back to the sleigh soon-ish, Edmund would be sure to hear about it, and as much as Aidan didn't want to leave this guy, almost nothing was worth one of Edmund's interminable lectures.

"I guess it is Christmas Eve." Aidan was undeniably smart, but the man in front of him left him grasping for something intelligent to say.

"You'd better get your boss Santa's favorites," the guy said with a smirk.

"Yeah," Aidan muttered, "anything less might be a breach of festivity."

Aidan knew *all* about breaches of festivity. It was Edmund's favorite topic.

The guy's eyes crinkled adorably. "Breach of festivity?" he wondered.

Aidan shot him a knowing look before turning down one of the aisles. Realized as his eyes alternatively searched through the brightly colored bags and boxes that he wasn't sure which cookies were Santa's favorite.

"Oreos are always a solid choice."

Aidan looked up in surprise and there was the guy, at the head of the aisle. He was tall, even taller than Aidan had realized he was, with long rangy legs in worn jeans, and a dark navy t-shirt that read, "Bah Humbug" on it.

A sentiment that resonated way more with Aidan than he could admit.

"Oreos?" Aidan had never had Oreos before. They weren't something the Tír na nÓg kitchens typically stocked, and whenever he and Ronan had snuck out of the compound, he hadn't been in the mood for sandwich cookies.

The guy shot him a strange look.

Probably because nobody else had ever questioned Oreos being a solid choice.

Aidan grabbed the biggest package on the shelf, not because he thought Sam really liked Oreos but because he wanted to see the guy smile again.

He was rewarded with a big grin, and it blew the rest of the thoughts right out of his head. There was something else that was supposed to go with the cookies, Edmund had been lecturing him about it for weeks, in case Santa felt like he needed a snack.

But under the powerful onslaught of the guy's presence, Aidan found the knowledge had just disappeared right out of his head.

Maybe if I see it, I'll remember it.

He headed towards the beverage coolers at the back of the store, and this time he wasn't surprised that the guy trailed after him.

"Looking for something in particular?" he asked as Aidan's eyes scanned the various beverages available.

There was a *lot*.

Aidan looked over at the guy. "Does everyone who comes in get such personal service?"

He had the audacity to flush, making him somehow, impossibly, even more handsome. And also more approachable. "Uh, it's been slow. I'm a bit bored," he admitted.

"Must be," Aidan said.

He'd been so preoccupied with the beverage choice, turning this way and that, craning his head to try to see the upper shelves, that he hadn't even noticed his hood slipping, and he didn't realize it had actually fallen down until he heard the guy's sharp intake of breath behind him.

"You're . . ."

Aidan turned, apprehension building in his stomach at the thought of Edmund's inevitable lecture—and at the thought of the guy's disgust.

Humans, as he'd learned over the years, didn't tend to like creatures who weren't like them.

And Aidan, though he mostly resembled a human, still wasn't human.

The ears, now exposed and flushed, were a dead freaking giveaway.

"You're . . ." the guy repeated, stuttering, but unlike what Aidan had feared, he didn't look upset. His expression was more fascinated than anything else. "You're an elf."

There was no point in denying it.

Aidan could have claimed it was a costume—a *really* good costume—but he knew how real his ears looked.

Because they *were* real.

"It *is* Christmas," Aidan acknowledged, tilting his head.

The guy laughed again, like Aidan had startled it right out of him. "I guess it is," he said. "You're here . . . you're here with Santa, aren't you? That's your boss."

Aidan clicked his tongue against the roof of his mouth. The secrecy that the elves protected fiercely, *especially* the North Pole elves, was crumbling by the moment. "You're pretty smart."

It was the guy's turn to shoot him an incredulous look, right in front of the various different kinds of Coke. *Orange Coke, really?* Aidan thought absently.

"It's not that big of a leap," he said wryly. "It's Christmas Eve. You're an elf. You're picking up cookies and . . ."

"And?" Aidan tapped his foot nervously against the linoleum floor. Hoped that the guy would tell him what freaking went with cookies so he could finish freaking out in peace. "Cookies and . . . ?"

It was hopeless to expect that even being the Christmas Savior was going to protect him from the backlash on this.

Edmund would never let him hear the end of it.

"And?" The guy looked confused. "Don't you know what goes with cookies? For *Santa*?"

"Of course I do. Maybe I'm just testing you," Aidan said snarkily. He was still unbearably attracted to the guy. But he also kinda wanted to throttle him. "After all, you're apparently the Scrooge in this scenario." He pointed to his t-shirt.

"You know about Scrooge?" the guy's eyes widened.

"Oh, please, he's got a really bad reputation," Aidan said. Probably no worse than his own would be when Edmund found out about his cluelessness.

"Huh, well, I can see that," the guy said thoughtfully. Then his gaze narrowed again. "If you know what Santa likes with his cookies, why are you still looking at sodas?"

"You really are more perceptive than most humans," Aidan said with a sniff.

He shrugged. "I do okay for myself."

But Aidan had seen the intelligence gleaming in his dark eyes, and he wasn't afraid, the way most ignorant humans might be, when confronted by something *other*.

Clearly he did a lot better than "okay."

"Did they send a clueless elf with Santa?" the guy teased, clearly not wanting to give up on his theory.

The theory that was, unfortunately, all too correct. This was something Aidan *knew* he knew, but between the attraction that had short-circuited his brain and the fear of discovery, and now this gentle teasing, he was flustered and scrambling for the right answer.

"I'm new," Aidan said stiffly.

"Huh," the guy said, clearly fascinated by this. "Why would they send a new elf with Santa? On Christmas Eve?"

"It's a long, annoying story," Aidan huffed. "I don't really want to talk about it. Are you going to tell me what Santa likes with his cookies or not?"

The guy smiled sweet and slow. It was different than all that charisma blasting Aidan, but somehow, he liked it even more. This smile didn't feel like the one the guy gave everyone; instead, it felt *personal*.

"Sure," he said. Then to Aidan's shock, he extended his hand. "The name's Dexter," he said. "Dexter Hawkins."

MERRY ELF-ING CHRISTMAS

Aidan looked at the hand. He wanted to take it, but how many more rules would he breaking if he did?

"What, are elves not allowed to introduce themselves?" Dexter frowned. "You do *have* a name, right? You're not just like . . . *Elf number six hundred and thirty-two*, right?"

"Of course I have a name," Aidan grumbled. "And no, not really on the introductions. We're not . . . you weren't supposed to know what I was."

Dexter's leisurely perusal from his feet, in their leather slippers, with their special nonslip nubbly soles, to his fleece-lined leggings, to his red tunic, barely covered by his fur-lined cloak, and then, finally, to his ears, which were *burning* by the end of this, meant his retort was not all that surprising.

"Was I supposed to think you were . . . *normal* in that getup?"

"It *is* Christmas," Aidan said. "You said it was."

"Yeah, I guess, I've seen stranger," Dexter said, rubbing his jaw with his hand. "Still, you're not exactly inconspicuous."

"I would have been in and out if . . ." Aidan stopped himself from saying *if you hadn't been so goddamned hot* just in time. "Well, if I'd remembered what Santa likes with his cookies."

Dexter gave an impatient wave, and Aidan trailed after him, to the very end of the beverage cooler. He reached up, grabbing a bottle off the top shelf. "Here," he said, handing it to Aidan. "Not sure that you could've reached it anyway. Not without help." He grinned at Aidan.

Aidan's fingers closed over the bottle of milk. He shifted it and decided, *what the hell, you're already in deep shit*. "Aidan," he said, reaching out with his hand, and this time Dexter took it, shaking it slowly and carefully, before letting it go.

"I didn't know they had Irish elves in the North Pole," Dexter said as Aidan followed him towards the front, towards the counter.

"I wasn't always a North Pole elf," Aidan admitted.

"You mentioned that," Dexter said, confirming Aidan's suspicion that this one had a mind like a steel trap, along with those soulful eyes that made him never want to leave.

Aidan glanced over to the counter, and saw textbooks piled there, alongside a notebook full of carefully written notes. Dexter's handwriting was impossibly neat, completely different than his own. Something about mass and density and he realized that Dexter was a student. "Yeah," Dexter said, noticing his stare, "I'm an engineering student. Working on my master's in mechanical engineering. I like to build things, not just advise cute elves on what Santa might like with his Oreos."

Aidan found himself going bright red. Not a great look with his red tunic, but he willed his embarrassment away.

He thought Dexter was absolutely smoking hot.

Why couldn't it be mutual?

It can't be mutual because you live in the North Pole, and you're literally Not Allowed to even talk to him, more than just a friendly hello. You're meant to never be seen, and not be heard.

"You have cash, right?"

Aidan's eyes flew up, meeting Dexter's. "Of course I do," he said. "What kind of elf would I be if I came into the world without its currency?"

"Hey, hey, it's cool, I just wanted to make sure. Otherwise, of course, this is for Santa. He can have whatever he wants. Not sure Mr. Husseini would believe me . . ."

"Who is Mr. Husseini?"

Dexter grinned brightly. "He owns this store, and a bunch of others, he's a great guy. Takes care of us, if you know what I mean? Not sure he believes in Santa, but if I told him it was important, he'd get it."

Aidan didn't know why it mattered to him one way or another that Dexter worked for someone who gave a shit, because he didn't *know* Dexter, not really. But he could still want good things for him, right?

Aidan might be an elf, but he wasn't a monster.

"Santa isn't used to people giving *him* gifts," Aidan said thoughtfully, but pulled out the wad of cash that Edmund had given him anyway. He didn't want Dexter to get in trouble with his boss, no matter how nice he was.

Plus, it was bad enough that Dexter knew the truth of Aidan's identity. It would be so much worse if he told Mr. Husseini.

He laid a bill on the counter. "Is this enough?" he asked.

Dexter stared at it.

"Uh, yeah," he said, "let me grab you some change. I think I have enough . . ."

While he was sorting through a bunch more bills in his register, Dexter glanced up. "Do you do this a lot?"

"Help Santa?" Aidan said in a teasing voice. "Just once a year."

"I mean, come into *our* world," Dexter said.

Aidan figured that Dexter already knew the worst of him. Why not tell him everything? "My friend Ronan and I used to sneak out of Tír na nÓg pretty regularly," he said, "because it was close to some towns. We could go grab a drink, socialize a bit, you know, just have some fun, but the North Pole? Not really a lot of friendly faces to be found up there. Definitely no pubs."

"So you can leave, then, if you wanted to," Dexter observed casually as he counted the money.

"It's not encouraged, no, but . . . there are always ways around the rules," Aidan admitted.

"And you watch movies," Dexter stated, laying the money on the counter. It was a lot more bills than the single one Aidan had handed him.

Every time he underestimated Dexter, he was surprised. "How do you know that?"

Dexter gestured to his shirt. "You know about Scrooge."

"Technically," Aidan said, shooting him a lopsided grin, "that was a *book* first."

"Right, right, but you do, right? Do you guys have technology up in the North Pole? You must, how else would you deliver all those presents?"

"Magic?"

Dexter's eyes gleamed.

And Aidan realized, horribly, that he was having more fun than he had since he'd moved to the North Pole. More fun, even, than a lot of those tipsy, joyous nights sneaking out with Ronan.

"Do you have magic?" he asked.

"We all have a little magic. Not as much as Santa does, but a little," Aidan admitted. "But yeah, we do have technology. Makes things easier."

"What about a phone number? Do you have one of those?" Dexter's questions were so casual, so haphazardly inserted into the conversation that for a second, Aidan didn't realize what he was asking.

Then he did and he stared at Dexter. "You want to talk to me?"

Dexter shrugged. "You're the first elf I've ever met. Why wouldn't I?"

It was more than that though. It was the chemistry crackling between them, stronger than Aidan had ever experienced before.

"No phones, not in the way you'd think," Aidan said slowly, "but . . ." He hesitated for a second. Edmund would kill him. Slowly. But there wasn't any reason for him to find out. "But I do have an email address?"

Dexter's smile was infectious. "Yeah?"

Aidan nodded.

Flipping the receipt, Dexter slid the pen he'd been using to make notes, alongside the paper, towards Aidan. "Well," he said, "I'd like to formally request your email address, then."

"Formally?" Aidan raised an eyebrow.

"I don't want . . . I know you're not the same as us. Maybe not with the same . . . well, I don't want to make you uncomfortable." Dexter suddenly seemed uncomfortable himself. "I don't know if you were *really* flirting with me or just . . . being an elf. I've never met an elf before."

Suddenly, Aidan realized why Dexter suddenly seemed so awkward. "You're afraid I don't like men, not like that. Is that not common here?"

"Uh, well, not *common* necessarily, but some people don't like to talk about it . . ." Dexter trailed off.

Aidan didn't think, he just reached out and put his hand on Dexter's, lying right there, on the counter, between the Oreos and the stack of bills. His hand was big and warm, and Aidan felt the heat of it blast right through him. He hadn't really been warm since Ireland and now . . . well, he was freaking steaming hot.

"Uh," Dexter said, his eyes widening. He'd felt it too, then. It wasn't just Aidan, and if he wanted his email address . . .

It was undeniable this whole attraction thing was mutual.

Aidan squeezed his hand gently and then picked up the pen. Scribbled down his email address. "There," he said softly, "now we can talk."

Dexter's gaze was intent. "Are you going to get in trouble for talking to me?"

Yes, probably, and I don't care. It'll be worth every second of Edmund's interminable lectures.

"It'll be fine," Aidan said breezily. "I'll just say you're some kind of festivity distributor."

Dexter raised an eyebrow. "A festivity distributor, I . . ."

"It'll be fine, just fine," Aidan interrupted with a forced kind of cheerfulness that he didn't really feel. It probably wouldn't be fine. And Santa was going to be wondering what he'd been up to. He'd have to figure out something to say to him, to excuse all the time he'd spent in here.

But even if it wasn't fine, he'd have this moment, the last twenty minutes he'd spent with Dexter of the kind eyes and the handsome face, and the body he'd like to . . . well, and he'd have whatever emails they managed to exchange. Even if they never exchanged any . . . it would still be worth it.

Aidan believed that to the soles of his pointy shoes.

"If you think so," Dexter said slowly.

"I do," Aidan said. "I . . . I hope you do email me."

Dexter smiled slow, and it sparked up Aidan's spine. "I plan on it."

"Okay." Aidan couldn't delay any longer. He picked up the milk and cookies from the counter.

"Your change?" Dexter said, pushing the stack of bills towards him. "You don't want to forget that."

"Keep it," Aidan said suddenly. "I . . . we don't really use it up in the North Pole and I know you do. Maybe you could . . . consider it . . . consider it a gift from Santa."

"Thanks, I shouldn't take it, but . . ." Dexter hesitated. "However, I could use it, so I will. But only if you let me consider it a gift from *you*."

Aidan felt a bit breathless. "Yes, okay, you can do that."

"Alright, then," Dexter said, and suddenly his smile was a bit less dim. "You have to go, don't you?"

"Yes." He really should have left ages ago.

"I understand." From the look in his eyes, Aidan knew he understood. But that didn't make it any easier to turn and walk out the door.

The icy air hit him like a blast of reality as he set foot outside.

Hurrying towards the sleigh, he found Sam in the alley, just as he'd left him, his booted feet stretched out in front of him, his head thrown back as he whistled "God Rest Ye Merry Gentlemen," in a bright, happy tone.

"Oh good, Aidan, you're back," he said as Aidan climbed into the sleigh, depositing his purchases onto the seat between them.

Aidan waited, expectantly, for the inevitable comment about how long it had taken him. But Sam didn't say a word, instead he just ripped open the Oreo package, and munched happily away on a handful of cookies.

"Here," Aidan said, and handed him the plastic bottle of milk.

"Oh," Sam said with a delighted voice, "you got me chocolate milk. How did you know it's my favorite? Everyone, even Edmund, insists for 'Christmas purity' that I drink white, but you know what? Chocolate's always better."

"I . . . uh . . ." Aidan hesitated. It hadn't been him who'd picked the chocolate milk. That had been all Dexter.

Even still, he felt a warm burning in his stomach just at the thought of him.

"It's alright," Sam said, giving him a crinkly-eyed smile and a reassuring pat on the shoulder, "you young elves are free to keep your secrets, as long as it gets me Oreos and chocolate milk."

"We . . . we are?" Aidan was surprised.

Sam's blue eyes were twinkling in his lined, kind face. "Well, of course you are, Aidan. You're not my employee, you're my friend."

Aidan, for the very first time, realized why it was that so many elves followed Santa with such a fiercely loving devotion.

Because he loved each of them back.

And that warmth, well, it grew a little bit.

Not enough to keep him warm once Santa lifted off in the sleigh, and a blast of chilled air snuck right up the back of his cloak again. But the memory of it, well, Aidan wasn't going to forget that for a very long time.

Chapter Two

Dexter watched the door close behind him, and for a long moment, couldn't quite tear his eyes away from it, because maybe Aidan would come back.

After all, he'd shown up out of nowhere, a welcome shock to Dex's system, used to the same kind of customers, the same kind of people, the same kind of conversations. So why wouldn't he just appear again? *Magically*, a voice inside him added slyly.

But after a minute, and then another, and then a third, the door remained stubbornly closed.

Dexter let out a frustrated sigh, and before he could stop himself, pinched his arm hard.

Yep, he was definitely awake. That had definitely just happened, and not just because there was a pile of cash on the counter and a slip of paper with Aidan's email address written on it in neat, careful letters.

Proof he'd been here.

Proof he'd existed, and he wasn't just a stray figment of Dex's imagination, sick of studying and bored with how slow and quiet his night had been.

Aidan had come in, all twinkling green eyes and tousled blond hair, with that absolutely ridiculous outfit, even if it *was* Christmas, and Dexter had been entranced, even if he hadn't expected to be.

Initially, Aidan had been an irresistible combination of puzzled charm and inherent mystery, and then he'd smiled, and Dexter had found his heart beating just a little bit faster.

Found himself trying to make him stay a little longer.

He'd wanted to know so much more about Aidan. Not just about his job, and what elves *did*, and what the North Pole was like, and *oh my God*, what about Santa, but what Aidan sounded like when he laughed. What he looked like when he was sleepy and happy and sad and what he sounded like when he was turned on.

But there hadn't been any time for that.

He finally found someone he really *liked* and of course they were basically unavailable.

Except . . . Dexter glanced down at the email that Aidan had written on the back of the receipt.

He shook off his frustration and pulled his tablet out of his bag, and set it up on the counter. Made sure he was connected to the Wi-Fi and opened up his email. Typed in Aidan's address and, for now, left the subject blank.

Subjects were hard. He'd figure that out later.

Dear Aidan, he wrote, and then his fingers hesitated on the keys.

Was that too formal?

Should he start with just "Aidan," instead? Or skip the name altogether and settle for something more casual and universal like "hi," or "hey"?

Dexter made a frustrated sound under his breath.

He wanted to do this right, but he didn't know what the right way was.

He started again.

Aidan, he typed, and then froze again. He'd been all hung up on the greeting, but now this was even worse.

He knew what he wanted to say.

It's been ten minutes since you left, and it's the longest ten minutes I can remember.

But that was so emotional and almost *silly*, that Dex rejected it.

Tried something else.

I hope, he wrote, **that the rest of your deliveries go smoothly, and that you get back to the North Pole safe and sound.**

Dex made another disgruntled sound.

He sounded like an uptight prick.

Not who he was, not at all, and not the impression he wanted to give Aidan either.

Elves were playful and fun, right? Or was that just the way Hollywood had portrayed them?

The last thing Dexter wanted to do was fall into stereotypes. But then, Aidan *had* smiled at him a bunch. He also remembered a very distinct twinkle in his eyes. He'd been amused. Having a good time.

Because he did that all the time?

Or because of Dexter?

You're not that funny, he told himself firmly. *You know that's true.*

He deleted the line he'd written one letter at a time, hitting the backspace key harder than he needed to.

Be honest with the guy, but not too honest. This suggestion sounded like something his friend Jonathan would say.

"I can do this," Dexter said out loud, ignoring the butterflies in his stomach. What if he messed this up? And Aidan never replied?

That would suck. But it would not be the end of the world.

"Plenty of elves in the sea," Dexter mumbled under his breath as he started typing again.

I've tried to start this email to you about half a dozen times now, and I can't figure out why. Maybe because I'm still thinking about you and you've only been out of the store for approximately half an hour. Or maybe because I've never emailed an elf before.

I'm not sure which, but I've had some pretty terrible openings, and I finally decided, I'm just going to have to go with what my nana said (and also, incidentally, Mr. Husseini), which is that honesty is always the best policy.

I really liked meeting you.

I really liked talking to you.

That you've got pointy ears and live in the North Pole is definitely different but it doesn't make me like you any less—though the North Pole thing could put a cramp in some things. I know we don't know each other yet, but that's why I was so relieved you had an email address: because I want to know you and I guess this is the only way I can right now.

It was quiet after you left. Honestly, it was quiet before you came. I was studying for my Product Management in Industry class, minding my own business, glad that I had helped Mr. Husseini out of a tight spot and agreed to work on Christmas Eve when you walked in.

Saved me from a whole evening of boredom, actually, because since you left, I've spent all this time trying to write this stupid email.

Hopefully, you don't think I'm a dork. Or if you do, that you don't judge. I haven't met an elf before and I'm a little starstruck.

I guess I should tell you a little bit about me.

I'm 25. I go to the University of Chicago. I'm getting a master's in mechanical engineering. Before you ask, yes, I've always liked taking things apart and putting them back together. Confused and annoyed my parents—and when they weren't around, the nannies. Yeah, I guess I should mention that, too.

I didn't see my parents a lot growing up. Even before the divorce.

I know you were wondering why I was working on Christmas Eve. Your reason is a lot better than mine.

Mine is because I cut my parents out of my life, because they never made me feel good, and whenever they made me feel bad, they thought they could buy me something to make it better. Which is why I'm working at Mr. Husseini's store—I have a trust, but I haven't ever touched it.

Let's see . . . what else? Now that I've made things super awkward by telling you all about how I don't get along with my parents, I guess you might want to know if I'm single.

I'm not dating anyone. I had a boyfriend in high school, but I think he just liked my big house and that he could come there whenever he wanted. We broke up my senior year. In college I've been too busy with class and work to really think about dating.

God, this part makes me sound really pathetic, doesn't it? Alone on Christmas Eve. Perennially single. I do have friends, I promise.

Jonathan, he's in my classes, he's probably my best friend. He's always pushing me to "put myself out there," whatever the hell that means. He'd probably be really happy I'm sending this email, but I won't tell him, because even though you were downplaying it, I could tell that I wasn't supposed to know who you really are.

I'm probably not supposed to be emailing you either. But what else is there to do up in the North Pole except answer semi-desperate emails from strangers who wear Scrooge t-shirts unironically?

Don't answer that.

Actually—do answer that. I want to know what your life is like when you're up at the North Pole. Is it more *The Santa Clause* or *Arthur Christmas*? Or *Elf*?

Do you even know what those are?

Maybe I should be hoping that you don't.

Anyway—this is getting even more embarrassingly long, so I'll cut it off now, before I ramble any more and you definitely think I'm a dork.

I hope the rest of your deliveries went well, and that Santa enjoyed his Oreos.

Dexter

The one time Aidan had suggested to Edmund that Santa didn't really *need* the assistance of an elf in the sleigh, that the only reason Santa kept one around on Christmas Eve was for appearances, he'd been beyond offended.

But it was the truth.

Aidan didn't have much to do in the sleigh. Sam's magic summoned the gifts, and magic sent them down the chimneys or through mail slots or even through dryer vents. Not everyone these days had a fireplace, and they'd learned to be adaptable, at least according to Edmund.

Aidan had also made the mistake of bringing up the fact that Santa *going* to each and every house was not strictly necessary.

"Magic," he'd said, "is what summons the presents from the North Pole. And then Santa directs them to the right spot. Not the sleigh. Not really."

"Are you suggesting that we just summon gifts to everyone's house from the *North Pole*," Edmund had asked, aghast. "It's much easier this way, for Santa to keep it straight in his head, and less of a strain on his magic. The distance matters."

"Right," Aidan had agreed, even though he hadn't quite believed it.

Edmund had just finished bragging about how Santa was one of the most powerful magical beings in the world—so much more powerful than the leprechauns he'd just left at Tír na nÓg—so it was difficult for Aidan to accept that Santa wouldn't be capable of delivering gifts even from thousands of miles away.

The long and short of Santa's power was that it meant Aidan had very little to do.

He kept track of the list, though it was more of a symbolic gesture than anything else, and he did things like fetch Sam milk and cookies.

Dexter.

He'd been trying not to think about him the whole night, but it had been hard to resist, because he hadn't much else to occupy his mind.

His time had been pretty evenly split between deciding that Edmund was just plain wrong, and how much he hoped that Dexter would send him an email.

Then they were finally heading back to the North Pole, Sam doing a little fancy flying once they were through the magical protective barrier that meant satellites and nosy researchers wouldn't ever see that this desolate plain was actually a bustling city, sending up a cheer from the assembled elves on the ground.

It was, Aidan conceded, a little exciting, even if his balls were still frozen solid.

Edmund was waiting for them the moment Sam pulled the sleigh into the large warehouse garage where the sleigh was kept and maintained.

"Merry Christmas!" Sam bellowed and Edmund clapped alongside the other elves, losing, for a moment, that constipated look to his expression.

Christmas, the only holiday that even Edmund can't be insufferable during.

"Aidan," Edmund said, after he descended from the sleigh after Sam. "A moment of your time, please."

Sam was offering high fives and hugs and exchanging holiday greetings with all the elves, who looked thrilled to be able to be here to welcome the sleigh.

Did Aidan get any of those? No. He got Edmund's annoyingly official voice.

Guess you were wrong, Edmund can still manage it, even during Christmas.

"What?" Aidan asked. He really wanted to go back to his room, see if Dexter had emailed him.

"Well, how was it?" Edmund asked impatiently.

"It was fine," Aidan said. "Everything went fine."

Edmund did not look convinced. "First time out with Santa on Christmas Eve and it was . . . *fine*?"

"Uh." Aidan realized his error. "Uh, it was good? Really good. No problems. No . . . uh . . . breaches of festivity, not tonight."

"I'm glad," Edmund said cautiously, like he didn't quite believe Aidan.

Edmund was painfully perceptive, because *yeah*, there had been a huge breach of festivity.

Dexter.

"If that's all . . ." Aidan said, trailing off.

Edmund harrumphed. "If you must leave, then I suppose you can. But remember, there's the gala tonight."

Aidan must have looked blank at this.

"The *Christmas Gala?*" Edmund repeated. Then just shook his head. "I keep forgetting you're new to the North Pole. You won't be able to miss it. You're practically the star of the show. Usually starts at dusk."

Aidan considered asking him what would happen if he was up to his eyeballs with Christmas gaiety, but he could only imagine what Edmund would say to that, so he kept his mouth shut and just nodded.

If Dexter had actually emailed him, maybe he'd be in the mood to celebrate some more.

He lived in one of the big apartment buildings for all the single elves, the ones who didn't have families and who hadn't earned one of the small cottages dotted across the snowy landscape.

There was a huge group of celebrating elves in the foyer, and he skirted around them, taking the stairs at a breathless pace instead of waiting for the elevator.

The door was keyed to his biometrics—a neat bit of science and magic that Aidan could only imagine that Dexter would love.

He shut the door behind him, and headed straight for his tablet. He'd been issued one as soon as he'd arrived at the North Pole.

He'd still had the one he'd been given at Tír na nÓg, but Edmund had sniffed at their technology, claiming that it wouldn't be able to withstand the temperatures up here.

Aidan flicked it on, and quickly navigated, his breath catching in his throat, to his email inbox.

And there it was.

An email, sent from a dhawkins357@illinois.chi.edu.

His fingers trembled as he clicked on the screen, opening the email.

He read the email once, then twice, and then a third time.

Collapsing onto the chair in front of him, he perused it a fourth time, warmth spreading through his chest at Dexter's words.

He *liked* him. He didn't care that he was an elf. And he was *single*.

Even more astounding, Dexter wanted to *know* him.

Well, he could do that.

His fingers still shaking, he clicked reply and began to type.

Dexter,

I tried really hard the rest of the flight to not wonder if you'd email me. I'm so happy you did.

I don't think you're a dork. Or starstruck. At least I hope you're not starstruck, because there's nothing special about me, no matter what anyone—especially Edmund—says. Though that's a story for another time.

I guess I should tell you something about me, too.

I'm quite a bit older than 25, though I guess I don't look it. Us elves are very long-lived. Something about the magic in the air or on the ground. I've never paid good attention to the specifics, but I can find out if you're interested.

I am also single.

I work for . . . well, you know.

Sam is what he likes me to call him. Santa is more of an honorary title. His family is very long-lived but there's been

Santas around forever. The rest of the elves call him Santa, like he's some kind of mythological figurehead—oh wait, I guess he is—but I get the privilege of calling him by his first name.

Why is that?

Well, that's probably better for another day and another email, but it's why I'm new to the North Pole, and why I was picked to assist Santa in my first year.

Edmund, the head of the North Pole elves, isn't very happy about it. There's a lot of things I don't really like about the North Pole, but he's definitely top five.

Maybe he's angry I took his job.

Because I did.

Like I said, story for another email, especially because there's so much you said I want to talk about, and I'm already late for this stupid Christmas Gala that Edmund is insisting I attend.

What is the North Pole like?

Well, it's not like *The Santa Clause*.

North Pole elves aren't so into contracts.

Besides, Bernard is a walk in the park compared to Edmund.

Maybe even a walk across a freaking frozen tundra.

Anyway, no, it's not like *The Santa Clause*. Elves smile, but not that much (it would be creepy if they did!), and Sam's too agile to fall off a roof. Also, Edmund would lose his shit if he had to find a new Santa.

Especially a Santa in advertising.

Though if he did, at least Santa would be more into all his branding-improvement plans. Yes, even in the North Pole we have corporate bullshit.

There's lots more to say about the North Pole, but I'll leave it there, for now.

Except to say, your email was the best Christmas gift I got this year.

Actually . . . now that I think about it, my only Christmas gift this year? It's kind of fucked up how North Pole elves are too busy trying to deliver Christmas cheer to everyone else to ever really worry about it for themselves.

Anyway, I was really happy, that's what I'm trying to say.

Hope to hear from you soon (and afraid this closing sounds very needy),

Aidan

From: dhawkins357@illinois.chi.edu
To: aidan@npenterprises.com
Date: December 26, 2021, 9:26 PM

Aidan,

I'm glad elves smile, though not as much as they do in *The Santa Clause*, because you're right, *creepy*.

I knew that though, already, because *you* smiled.

Not at first. But when you did? I haven't been able to stop thinking about it.

Here's the thing: I knew you were special and different when you smiled at me for the first time. You said secrecy in the elf world is a big deal, but here's the thing probably nobody's ever told you because it sounds like you've all been avoiding humans and never asking their opinion—which, really, can't blame you for that one, we're idiots—but there's something different about you.

But then you're the only elf I've ever met, and maybe elves aren't all like you. I'm definitely not like other humans.

I like this hypothesis, especially when I consider what you've said about Edmund.

But back to you—I knew there was something unique about you long before your hood fell down and I saw your ears. And it wasn't that Christmas Elf getup you were wearing either. Though, really, if you're so worried about secrecy, there's always blending in? Maybe something to pass along to Edmund during one of your many branding meetings?

I've been thinking about this, and I knew it when you smiled.

It shone a light into a place inside me where it's been dark for a long time. So no matter what happens, thank you for that.

You said a lot about what the North Pole *isn't* like, but you didn't really say what it *is* like. So not *The Santa Clause*. I admit that based on your description, Edmund doesn't sound very Bernard-esque.

Jonathan's been wondering why I'm watching all these Christmas movies post-Christmas, but I haven't told him why yet.

Even if you'd told me that I could, I wouldn't know how to bring it up.

It isn't that he wouldn't believe me. Jonathan has more imagination than I do. Also, he's a certified Christmas nut. Maybe Edmund would like to hire *him* LOL.

But I like that this whole thing is just between us.

Unless, of course you've told someone, and if you have, I of course want to know, immediately, and what you said about me.

Dex (this is what my friends call me, and you're a friend)

———ele———

"You're literally grinning like you just won the lottery," Jonathan hissed under his breath as Dex finished typing his second email to Aidan. "Did that headhunter email you again?"

For a second, Dex didn't understand what Jonathan was saying. Headhunter? What headhunter? Aidan wasn't . . .

Then he realized that he must've looked excited and happy and like he fucking *felt*—which was full of joy—and Jonathan, who had no idea Aidan existed or that he'd even met someone, had assumed that he was like this because he'd received a killer job offer.

"No," Dexter said. "Not the headhunter."

Like any of the potential job offers he'd gotten would ever make him smile like he did over Aidan's words.

In fact, they'd all had the opposite effect.

Dex had gone into engineering because he'd always wanted an interesting problem to solve. So he'd never be bored. But the problems that the headhunters wanted him to fix?

Boring.

"Well, it was fucking *somebody*," Jonathan said insistently, sliding around the table at the library they'd been camped at for hours.

Dex had told himself that once he finished his notes for his Advanced Transport Phenomena class, he would allow himself to write back to Aidan.

Jonathan hadn't been quite ready to go yet when he had, so he'd used the extra time to start writing the email.

Not remembering, stupidly, that Jonathan would be able to spot the excitement in his expression in a heartbeat.

"Uh, not really anybody," Dexter lied, badly.

Jonathan made a face. "You're hiding something, and you're not even doing a good job of it."

"Maybe, okay maybe it *is* somebody," Dexter conceded. "But it's really early, and I'm not ready to talk about it yet."

"Who is it?" Jonathan asked, looking intrigued.

"That is the whole point of me saying I didn't want to talk about it yet, that it's still too early," Dex argued. "But it's someone I met at the store, actually. They're from out of town, so we're emailing."

"Romantic," Jonathan teased. "You gonna have cybersex with them?"

"Cybersex? What are you, from the AOL age?"

"I'm just saying, you guys emailing back and forth, that's something out of like . . . Jane fucking Austen or something."

Dexter rolled his eyes and snapped his tablet shut. "Jane Austen didn't *have* email," he pointed out. "Come on, let's find some food. I'm starving."

From: aidan@npenterprises.com
To: dhawkins357@illinois.chi.edu
Date: December 30, 2021, 6:57 AM
Dex,
That's the nicest thing anyone's ever said to me.

And that's including the other day when Belinda actually mounted a half-hearted defense of me in the staff meeting. To Edmund's credit, I haven't been studying the sleigh diagrams as much as I probably should.

What can I say? They make me nod off quicker than *It's a Wonderful Life*. Not a bad movie, despite having no elves, but it's so damn long.

Puts me right to sleep, proving I'm not even the semi-qualified North Pole elf that Edmund keeps accusing me of being.

Maybe if you were studying the sleigh plans with me, I'd be more interested.

I have a pretty good imagination; I can see it now. Us, bent over my desk, heads close together, you pointing to specific spots on the plans and explaining to me how it works. I wouldn't be surprised if you were a little surprised once or twice—the sleigh is an engineering marvel, even if I don't really understand the plans, but it's also built with magic. But then I'd turn my head just as you'd turn yours and . . . well, I remember what you said about imagination, but I think yours is good enough to help fill in the rest.

I wouldn't even say it but I've been thinking about it.

Can't stop thinking about it, to be honest.

Maybe that's why I'm sitting here daydreaming about kissing you, and writing this email and not being a good North Pole elf and figuring out exactly how to fix the sleigh should it break down mid-delivery.

Even if it did, I wouldn't be the first person to fix it, anyway. There's a long list of options before we even get to me. Which . . . frankly that's a good thing.

Still, Edmund keeps reminding me there's only twelve months left til Christmas Eve.

Like I need the reminder.

Aidan

From: dhawkins357@illinois.chi.edu
To: aidan@npenterprises.com
Date: December 31, 2021, 11:12 AM

Aidan,

By the time I'd be finished with you, you'd not only have a thorough working knowledge of the sleigh, you'd be thoroughly utterly kissed.

Just pointing that out.

A few days back, Jonathan demanded to know why I've been so distracted.

He's right.

I'm daydreaming all the time.

About you.

We've been emailing since Christmas and it feels silly to say this, but I'm going to say it anyway.

I can't believe it's only been a week, and dozens and dozens of emails since I met you, but I feel like I'm getting to know you, the real you, and the more I learn, the more I like.

Your emails make me smile, they make me laugh, they make me wish you were right here, next to me.

Dex

"Aidan, *please*, you're not even paying attention." Edmund sounded annoyed.

Maybe justifiably.

Aidan looked up, feeling guilt shoot through him, because he *hadn't* been paying attention.

He'd been scrolling back through pages and pages in his inbox of emails he and Dex had exchanged during the last few weeks.

Some of them were longer, like actual real messages. Some of them were short, just a sentence or two long. There were so many of them, a handful of them were grouped in clusters, since they'd actually replied to each other, answered questions or discussed specific events. For example, the one on his screen now read, "PS I really hate Edmund."

Aidan clicked out of that one really quickly before Edmund actually looked at his screen and *read* it and he was in even more trouble.

Dexter wasn't wrong. And he wasn't alone.

Aidan was daydreaming all the time, too.

At first, he hadn't liked the North Pole because it was cold as hell, and because everyone—except Edmund, of course—kept talking to him in that annoyingly worshipful way, but now he didn't like it because it was too goddamned far away from Chicago.

"Sorry," he said sincerely. "Sorry, I wasn't paying attention."

"No," Edmund huffed. "You weren't. I'm not giving this presentation for my own edification. I, and for the record, everyone else in this room, know all about the historical, cultural, and mythological implications of Santa."

"Right."

They'd all learned this when they were practically in the cradle.

It was just Aidan who was behind.

Just Aidan who was clueless.

He genuinely cared about Dex. That wasn't up for debate. But had he been using him to distract himself from the very real and very shitty situation that he was in?

Maybe, a little.

———

From: aidan@npenterprises.com

To: dhawkins357@illinois.chi.edu

Date: January 28, 2022, 7:13 PM

Dex,

I know in a lot of our emails we just talk about random shit that happens during our days. I complain about Edmund and the fucking snow a lot. You tell me funny stories about Jonathan, about your professors, about your classes, sometimes about Mr. Husseini. Sometimes we talk what-ifs.

That's not what this email is going to be.

I said I would tell you this story, the story about how I came to the North Pole, at some point, and I guess it's *some point* now, because I'm feeling... well, I feel like shit.

You're always the person that makes me feel *less* like shit, so that's why I'm turning to you.

Before you, I wasn't really a rule breaker. Really, before the *North Pole* I wasn't a rule breaker. But the North Pole elves are so rigid, so fanatical in their Christmas devotion, sometimes it feels like there's no room to breathe.

For the first sixty-seven years of my life, I lived in Tír na nÓg, the elf community in Ireland. I was assistant to the vice president of Leprechaun Operations. It wasn't the best job, but I really liked it. Mr. O'Callaghan, my boss, was smart and he listened to me when I had good ideas, and there was nothing more exciting than tracking magical patterns through the atmosphere and predicting when we'd get a rainbow touchdown.

My best friend Ronan and I snuck out, sometimes, because Tír na nÓg was close enough to cities that we could grab a drink at the local pub and be back before anyone was the wiser.

Now? I'm in the middle of a fucking frozen tundra, and I hate it.

I don't even know why I'm here.

Actually.

That's not true.

I know exactly why I'm here. I'm here because I was born under the right (but more like the wrong) star.

North Pole elves are weirdly fanatical about prophecies. Don't ask me why. I haven't actually *asked* because frankly I'm afraid to hear the answer. But they are, and about four hundred years ago, a famous North Pole elf seer named Grace predicted that at some point in the future, an elf son born under the waxing crescent of the North Star, to an elf of taller stature and an elf of renowned kindness, would save Christmas.

They've been waiting for the Christmas Savior for over four hundred years. They always assumed that the Christmas Savior would be born in the North Pole.

Which is why they never looked *outside* of the North Pole, until they did, and they figured out that the elf, well, the elf savior is me.

Yep, I'm the Elf Who Will Save Christmas.

Weak cheer

The discovery that this magical elf savior was me meant that I had to leave Tír na nÓg, and that I had to move to the North Pole.

I think that's why Edmund is so hard on me. Wanting me to absorb a whole lifetime's worth of North Pole culture and Christmas joy in a few months.

It's not their fault that I just don't have it in me or that I don't care about the same things they care about.

Even if you (or Mr. Husseini) don't have a special nugget of wisdom to give, I just . . . wanted to tell you. Not just because telling you helps me breathe a little easier and feel slightly less like the guilt is going to eat me alive, but because I'm going to try. And it might help if someone held me accountable.

Will you do that for me?

Aidan

From: dhawkins357@illinois.chi.edu
  To: aidan@npenterprises.com
  Date: January 28, 2022, 9:39 PM
  Aidan,

Whatever you need, I'm there for you.

I'm grateful you shared your story. It makes me feel a little closer to you, even though we're a couple thousand miles away from each other.

I can't imagine what you've been through these last few months, but I'm glad I was able to make it a little easier.

You've made this really hard year here easier for me too. I don't know what I'd do if I couldn't check my inbox every morning and every night.

I look forward to every email you send me.

Even the ones that say just that you hate Edmund.

Or the ones that talk about how many blankets you need on your bed.

Or how *Bad Santa* is an abomination and shouldn't be considered a Christmas film (agreed, BTW).

Or how you wish that the Valentine's elves would focus less on commercialism and more on the spirit of the holiday (maybe something to suggest to Edmund so you can watch his head explode with the implications).

Basically—I just enjoy you being you.

No matter how you do it.

Dex

Chapter Three

From: dhawkins357@illinois.chi.edu
To: aidan@npenterprises.com
Date: March 17, 2022, 6:56 AM
Aidan,

I know today is going to be a weird day for you, and I want you to know that I'm here, thinking about you, and if you need to talk or if you don't—that's all fine.

When I put on a green t-shirt this morning, I could almost imagine the face you'd make.

Yes, it's a very stupid tradition.

Yes, it doesn't mean anything.

Why am I still doing it even though you've made it clear that none of the Tír na nÓg elves give a shit about me wearing green on St. Patrick's Day?

I guess it makes me feel a little bit closer to you, and I'll take that.

Dex

"You're not wearing green today," Belinda asked in a low voice, when Aidan walked into the biggest conference room for their monthly "all elves" meeting.

Aidan had been dreading it since he'd realized that his least favorite meeting of the month happened to fall on the holiday that had once meant everything to him.

Now?

He kept being told that he'd learn to love Christmas the way he'd loved St. Patrick's Day, but when he'd woken up this morning without Ronan, without Mr. O'Callaghan passing him a green beer and a handful of gold-wrapped chocolate coins, he knew he wasn't close yet.

He'd gotten ready with a weird ache in his chest, like a hole had been burrowed out of it.

The only thing that had come close to lifting his spirits this morning was the email from Dex.

Even he'd worn green today. All the other elves he'd seen were too.

Aidan had told Dexter once that elves only half-heartedly celebrated other holidays, at least the elves in Tír na nÓg had rarely thrown themselves into celebrating Christmas (leaving him at a distinct disadvantage when he'd moved to the North Pole), Valentine's Day or All Hallows' Eve.

Dex had expressed surprise at this, and had told him that maybe the North Pole elves would surprise him.

So far, they hadn't.

They'd been exactly what Aidan had expected. Wild about Christmas. Barely putting in any effort for Valentine's Day—which was fine by him, since he found the holiday increasingly commercialized; he'd wondered what the Cupid elves' staff meetings were like—and so far, it seemed that St. Patrick's Day would go by much the same way.

But the one thing he hadn't expected was the sea of green tunics.

"I'm not a Tír na nÓg elf anymore," Aidan told Belinda stiffly. Maybe he was being a little bit rude, considering she'd been one of the few elves who'd actually tried to befriend him instead of putting him on a pedestal.

"Yeah, well, green is *also* a color that St. Patrick's shares with Christmas," Belinda offered quietly. "So that's probably why it's popular."

"Of course," Aidan said, barely refraining from rolling his eyes.

"I think it'd be hard to come here and be expected to be different, after all those years," Belinda said as they walked down the stairs in the big amphitheater-style room.

It was the first time that anyone had expressed even the tiniest bit of understanding since he'd arrived, almost six months ago.

"Here," Aidan said, indicating a row midway through the room. "We should sit here."

Belinda looked surprised. "You don't want to sit in the front? But you *could,* you're . . ."

"Please, for the love of God, don't say it," Aidan grumbled, holding up a hand. "Maybe I could, but . . . like you just said: I can't just *be* different because the North Pole elves decided I'm their precious savior."

Belinda nodded. She had dark curls and kind eyes and he had wondered, ever since meeting her, how on earth she'd ended up working for Edmund.

"We didn't *decide,*" she added, shooting him a reprimanding look. "It was more than that."

"I know," Aidan said morosely. He'd known this day would be hard. This was the first St. Patrick's Day he'd spent away from Tír na nÓg, but it was hitting him harder than he'd expected, even with Dex's email to soften the sting. "If it had just been that, maybe I could've figured out a way to stay in Ireland."

Belinda patted him on the knee. "It's not so bad here, right?"

"You mean, other than the 'freezing tundra' part?" Aidan questioned. "It's actually not, really, I'm just not used to sticking inside the magical barrier."

"You *left* Tír na nÓg?" Belinda's intake of breath was swift. "Really?"

"Sometimes." Aidan shrugged. "The towns were a lot closer and we were careful, but a lot of elves did it, actually. Being here makes me feel a little . . . claustrophobic, I guess."

"Hey, Edmund's management style would make anyone feel that way," Belinda said, teasing gently.

"You really think so?" Aidan was surprised. It often felt like he was the only one who chafed under Edmund's leadership, probably because he was so often doing and saying the wrong thing, not having been steeped in hundreds of years of Christmas tradition.

"He's forgotten how to breathe," Belinda said.

Aidan didn't quite know what that meant. "And you're going to force him to remember?"

Belinda laughed, but he could tell from her thoughtful expression that she was considering it. "I'm not sure I'm the right person for that particular job."

"I'm not sure there's anyone else," Aidan pointed out bluntly.

She just shrugged as Edmund took to the front podium to start the meeting. "I guess we'll see."

Aidan kept quiet for almost the entirety of the meeting, until Edmund reluctantly opened up the floor to questions and suggestions.

Aidan's was the first hand up, before he'd even really considered what he was going to say.

He should be used to the wave of gasps and then complete and total awed silence that always accompanied him speaking or even sometimes just *appearing*. It was annoying, and as far as Aidan knew, it was just plain wrong.

Maybe he would save Christmas someday.

But that didn't mean he was a figure to be both adored and feared.

He was just an elf.

"I was thinking that maybe we should start some optional trips outside the magical sphere," Aidan said casually, like what he was suggesting didn't go against pretty much every law of elf-kind. *Stay out of sight, and definitely don't mix with humans.*

Another breathless gasp went through the audience in response to his suggestion.

"Are you . . ." Edmund looked like he was considering crawling through about a hundred elves to Aidan and then squeezing the life out of him, slowly. "Are you suggesting that we go out into the *human world*?"

"I'm saying that locking ourselves away in the magical sphere does nobody any favors," Aidan said brazenly. "We need some freedom. We need a fresh influx of ideas. We're stagnating away here, talking to just ourselves. We're running in freaking circles here."

Edmund leaned forward on the podium. "And you think this, after only being here for a few months?"

"I have a different perspective," Aidan said stubbornly, "because I *have* been here for only a few months."

"Well, it's an idea," Edmund said, shooting him an indulgent, patronizing smile. "We'll consider it."

Aidan knew he wouldn't.

But then he'd already anticipated this. The point of making his suggestion hadn't been to get Edmund to agree now. It had been to air it publicly.

To make everyone start to wonder if maybe the Christmas Savior knew something that the head of the North Pole elves did not.

He'd discussed it with Dex, over the last few weeks, and he'd suggested that potentially even bringing it up might help cause some positive change.

Aidan hadn't wanted to say it explicitly, but he'd felt it, deep down.

If he could pull this off . . . then he might get to see Dex sooner than next Christmas.

He might get to see him for more than ten minutes.

And that . . . well, that, despite everything else, more than the cold or the feeling of being trapped or the endless Christmas cheer . . . might make this whole thing worth it.

From: dhawkins357@illinois.chi.edu

To: aidan@npenterprises.com

Date: June 1, 2022, 4:27 PM

I know you're frustrated that it's been three months and Edmund hasn't budged on his opinion of your idea to start offering trips to the human world, but change takes time, and it's not surprising that it's taking longer than you'd like, because well, you've mentioned maybe a hundred times how everyone is really stuck in a rut.

It's going to take time to get everyone out of it.

Especially Edmund.

Any more luck on the idea to enlist Belinda to soften Edmund up?

Sorry this is so short. I'm studying for finals, Jonathan and I haven't left the library in what feels like days . . . kiss me, kill me, or save me.

Dex

From: aidan@npenterprises.com
To: dhawkins357@illinois.chi.edu
Date: June 2, 2022, 8:23 AM

Dex—

Wish I could knock on doors one and three. Just saying.

I thought about it last night.

Thought about it when I fell asleep, in my dreams, and when I woke up.

It's why I'm so freaking frustrated that this visitation plan isn't working faster.

You probably know it. I don't need to say it. But it hasn't even been six months since I stood in your store, and it's six months-plus til I will again.

It's too long.

Right now, Belinda and I are planning this big summer solstice celebration.

I've mentioned at least a dozen times to Belinda that I am confused why we're bothering to hold a "summer solstice" celebration when it's still cold as fuck outside. I don't think she's very happy with me right now, so the plan to use her to butter up Edmund might not fly right now.

Something to keep in the back pocket.

Aidan

From: dhawkins357@illinois.chi.edu
To: aidan@npenterprises.com
Date: June 2, 2022, 1:54 PM

A,

Summer solstice?

Why am I just hearing about this now?

D

From: aidan@npenterprises.com
To: dhawkins357@illinois.chi.edu
Date: June 2, 2022, 8:18 PM

Probably because I'm annoyed with myself.

You know I've been trying to get more into this whole Christmas merriment thing. Trying to understand why the other North Pole elves are so into it.

It hasn't even been going badly—Edmund's stubbornness notwithstanding—but I thought I had another few months before I had to officially gear up for the beginning of the "Christmas season."

I've been enjoying hot cocoa. It does help with all those freezing drafts.

I learned all about the historical implications of Santa.

In my spare time, I'm embroidering my own stocking. It doesn't look very good, but when I'm finished with mine, I'm going to do one for you, too.

Annette has been teaching me all about decorating. How to appropriately scatter ornaments over an entire tree.

Billy gave me a class on cookie baking. My chocolate chip cookies are good now. The sugar cookies could still use some work.

I'm *very* into the implications of mistletoe, especially if you're the one standing under it.

I was really starting to, you know . . . not hate it . . . but then this summer solstice thing happened.

Yeah, you know how in all those Christmas movies, they talk about the North Pole celebrating Christmas all year round, that it's *always* Christmas at the North Pole? Well, they're not freaking wrong.

I don't know, I just think it would feel more special if we only had to do it for like . . . a quarter of the year, or something crazy like that.

Anyway, I found out today that this isn't really a summer solstice celebration.

It's more like a "halfway to Christmas" celebration.

I should've known better.

Nope, this is basically the Christmas Gala I attended last year, except *outside*.

And you know my stance on that.

Aidan

From: dhawkins357@illinois.chi.edu
To: aidan@npenterprises.com
Date: June 3, 2022, 6:57 AM

I'm intrigued by this idea of mistletoe.

Tell me more.

Dex

PS If I was there, you wouldn't need all those blankets—or the hot cocoa either. I'd keep you plenty warm.

From: aidan@npenterprises.com
To: dhawkins357@illinois.chi.edu
Date: June 3, 2022, 7:16 AM

If this is another way of trying to get me to tell you about my dreams, then think again.

You don't need any insider info to impress me.

I'm already impressed.

I'm already crazy about you.

Besides, even the worst first kiss would be the best one in the whole damn world—because it's with *you*.

A

"You're doing that weird smiling thing you do again, whenever you read this guy's emails," Jonathan said. It didn't even sound like he was complaining, necessarily, just observing.

By now Dex knew the smile well.

Knew because he'd seen it on his own face a handful of times, surprising himself a few times when he'd caught a glimpse of it in a passing window or a bathroom mirror.

Aidan made him laugh. He made him smile. He turned him inside out, effortlessly.

"Yeah, I probably am," Dex admitted wryly.

"You ever going to meet this guy again?" Jonathan wondered. "Seems like he's always traveling."

For fifteen minutes, tops, in about six months, and it's crazy but it might actually be worth it, after a year of pining.

"I hope so," Dexter said.

"I hope so too," Jonathan said, stretching out on the blanket he and Dex had set out in the park. It was a warm summer Saturday, and they both had no work and no class, so Dexter had insisted they get some actual fresh air.

Even Chicago air.

They'd played a little one-on-one soccer, popped open their cooler of beer, and were relaxing now, just enjoying the growing dusk.

That was when Dexter had glanced at his phone and seen Aidan's reply to his email, and according to his best friend, had smiled like the world was burning and he didn't give a shit.

"Are you saying that because the last guy who asked me out, I wouldn't even let him get the rest of the sentence out before turning him down?" Dexter wondered. Even though he knew that was only partially it.

"Yes," Jonathan said firmly. "That and more. You're a little obsessed with this guy, and you barely know him."

"I know him," Dex argued.

Sometimes it felt like he knew every thought and feeling that Aidan had ever had—and while he didn't *like* every single one, he understood them. Considered himself lucky and grateful that Aidan was willing to share all of them.

Was willing to listen to Dexter share in return.

He'd told things that he'd never told anyone, even Jonathan, and they'd known each other for years.

"You met him for ten minutes six months ago," Jonathan pointed out, not too kindly. "You don't know him."

"We've exchanged hundreds of emails," Dexter pointed out.

"That doesn't mean you know him. It means you're probably giving yourself carpal tunnel when you should be studying."

"I study," Dexter argued again.

Jonathan sighed. "Listen, it's cute, it's even a little romantic that you're so hung up on this guy. But is it realistic? How do you know he feels the same way?"

That was one thing Dexter had never questioned. He *knew* Aidan felt the same way he did. That burning ache, just under the skin. The way he wanted to see him right before he went to sleep. The way he wanted to kiss him good morning. The way he wanted to never stop hearing Aidan's words in his head.

The way he was desperate to get Aidan into his bed.

It was all mutual.

Dex would bet his life on that fact.

"I know he feels the same way," Dex said.

"You sure sound confident," Jonathan said wryly. "You guys ever do the cybersex thing?"

Dexter laughed. "No," he said. "I think that'd be weird, to do it before we even kiss?" Not that he hadn't been tempted. He had. On more than one occasion.

Jonathan punched him lightly in the shoulder, his expression morphing into something more like sympathy. "You *are* crazy about this guy," Jonathan said. "Who would've thunk it."

And, you don't even know the half of it, Dexter thought. *He's not even a guy, he's an elf, and he's trying to start a revolution in the North Pole so we can be together more.*

Maybe most people wouldn't consider that a particularly romantic gesture, but Dex knew Aidan, could just *tell* that yeah, part of his struggle to get the elves to listen to him was not only because he did genuinely think it would help morale, but that he was trying to make this connection into a viable relationship.

A way for them to spend more than fifteen minutes together, once a year.

"Someday," Jonathan continued, "I wanna meet him. Of course, for that to happen, *you'd* actually have to meet up with him."

"You will," Dexter promised, because if he'd learned anything about Aidan in the last six months, nothing would stop his elf when he was on a mission.

———ele———

From: dhawkins357@illinois.chi.edu
To: aidan@npenterprises.com
Date: September 9, 2022, 8:46 PM
Aidan,
Got another email today from yet another pushy headhunter.
Wants me for some super secret government project in California.
When I asked for details, nope, nada, zip, zilch.
For a second, I was almost interested, but then, when he refused to give me anything, I can't lie. I basically thought of the worst-case scenario.
Superweapons.
The Manhattan Project.
Robots who accidentally take over the world.
Space missiles.
Sometimes having an imagination in this industry is a curse, not a blessing.
Jonathan thinks I am being very stupid, holding out for a job that not only pays well, but will intrigue me and won't accidentally blow up the earth in the process.
He's probably right.
Maybe I'll become that eccentric homeless guy who is capable of taking an engine apart and putting it back together.
Dex

———ele———

From: aidan@npenterprises.com
To: dhawkins357@illinois.chi.edu
Date: September 10, 2022, 9:46 AM
Dex,

I'm with Jonathan on this one, though I can hardly fault you for being annoyed with corporate jobs rife with red tape when well . . . I'm in one right now and it annoys the hell out of me even when I try to let it go.

How was the first week of classes?

I've been helping Billy in the bakery, prepping about a million fruitcakes.

In my dreams, you're now accompanied by dancing dried fruit. You're welcome.

Aidan

—ele—

From: dhawkins357@illinois.chi.edu
To: aidan@npenterprises.com
Date: September 10, 2022, 2:31 PM

Dancing dried fruit?!?!?

Are you very sure that you aren't also sneaking some rum while you're helping Billy with the fruitcakes?

Classes are fine. I'm mainly focusing on my graduate project this year, I won't get into details because the details are bound to make your eyes glaze over, and you get enough of that from Edmund's meetings. But it should be a good year. I can't believe that I'm this close to graduating, finally, and figuring out what the heck to do for the rest of my life.

Yeah, 'cause that's not intimidating or terrifying at all.

Dex

—ele—

"Billy, you're with Finneas, right? You've been with him for awhile?"

Billy looked up from the batter he was mixing, his arm muscles tensing as he whisked the thickening mixture.

"Yeah," he said, nodding. "For a couple of years now."

Aidan thought so. He'd seen them together in the cafeteria multiple times, and Belinda had offhandedly mentioned once that they were on the waiting list for one of the cabins so they could finally move in together.

"You guys are cute together," Aidan said. Hoping he didn't sound awkward. Dreading that he did. Because he wanted to talk to Billy about his relationship.

He'd told Dex the truth when he'd said that same-sex couples in the elf world were not uncommon. He also knew that they were a lot more accepted than same-sex couples in the human world. Which really made Dexter's overtures towards him last Christmas even more surprising.

He'd taken a risk, by not only flirting with someone of the male sex but also someone who happened to be an elf.

It just made him like and respect Dex all the more for his courage.

Billy nodded absently, still mixing his batter. Aidan, on the other hand, was cutting his dried-up fruit a lot slower.

It was September now. They only had a few more months until they could see each other again. And Aidan already knew that he wasn't going to want to wait another twelve months. It was possible that Edmund might relent and let them start to plan outings, but that was by no means guaranteed.

Aidan (and Aidan's inconvenient feelings) had started to wonder if there were other plans to be made.

As the Christmas Savior he couldn't leave—even if he did, they'd track him down, Sam's magic would find him instantly—but there was nothing stopping Dex from leaving Chicago when he graduated and potentially moving to the North Pole.

You know, aside from the human thing.

And the Edmund thing.

And the North Pole thing.

The more that Aidan had thought about it, the more he was hesitant to suggest it. It was a lot to ask anyone to leave everything they knew behind.

Aidan, who didn't have any relationship experience, realized that he might want to talk to someone who *did*.

Billy, who ran the bakery, and was apparently in a long-term relationship with Finn, might be able to help him. Even better, in the last few months, Aidan had begun to almost consider him a friend.

Was that enough to ask his advice?

Well, Aidan was about to find out.

"How did you guys get together?" Aidan asked.

Billy raised an eyebrow. "You got your eye on someone?"

"Uh . . ." Aidan hesitated. "Well, kinda?"

"Is it Belinda?"

Aidan shook his head. "No, no, not Belinda. She's a friend. My only friend. Well, before you decided to give me the time of day."

Billy smiled. "We're friends, Aidan. I think most of the elves don't know what to make of you. You're different. And on top of that, you're the Savior."

"Yeah," Aidan grumped.

"As for Finn and me . . . well, we met here, we practically grew up together, and then our friendship turned into more, and we've been . . . well, I guess we've been together a few years now."

The situations did not seem even remotely similar, but Aidan forged on ahead because who else was he going to ask?

"Did you have any . . . roadblocks in your relationship?" Aidan asked, trying to sound casual. "Did you have to ask each other to give up anything to be together?"

Billy frowned. "Give up . . . what are you talking about, Aidan? Are you in love with someone back at Tír na nÓg? Is this what this is about?"

He definitely wasn't—but the question put the idea into his head. He couldn't tell Billy about Dex the human in Chicago. But he could ask Billy about a guy named Dexter from Tír na nÓg.

"Yeah, it's one of the reasons why I hated to leave," Aidan admitted.

Billy's expression morphed from confusion to instant sympathy. "Oh, that must've been tough. No wonder you haven't looked all that happy to be here. So, you're wondering . . . what . . . if it would be okay to ask your friend to move here, for you?"

"Yes." It wasn't a perfect comparison, but it was better than nothing.

"That is a big step," Billy conceded.

"That's why I'm afraid to ask. I'm asking him to give up so many things, his home, his friends, his work," Aidan said, "and to do that all for me."

"Could you talk him into a trial run?"

"No," Aidan said, setting his knife down. "I don't think that would work." It was going to be hard enough to persuade Edmund to accept a human in their midst. The only way to do it would be to reveal that Dexter *knew*—and that he knew a *lot*.

Once Edmund realized just how much Dex knew about the North Pole and the communities of elves across the globe, there'd be no going back.

"Hmmm, well, I think the best way to move forward is to be honest, Aidan," Billy said. "Tell your friend how you feel. Tell him how much you miss him. Tell him that you'd like to figure out how to build a relationship, but you can't do that unless he's here. Then, hate to say it, but the ball's going to be in his court."

"Right." Aidan also feared that if he said what he was thinking—what was increasingly in his heart—it might scare Dexter away.

It was one thing to exchange hundreds upon hundreds of emails over the course of a year. It was another thing entirely to invite him to live in the North Pole.

But in May, he'd be done with his master's program. He wasn't loving any of his job offers. And based on everything Aidan had heard him say, he knew Dex would be of use up here. Edmund would put him to work and likely never let him take a breath. Plus if he wanted imagination . . . well, no better place to find it than with a bunch of elves.

Aidan resolved. If Christmas Eve went as well as he hoped it would, then he would broach the subject in the new year.

From: dhawkins357@illinois.chi.edu

To: aidan@npenterprises.com

Date: October 31, 2022, 7:34 AM

Aidan,

Happy Halloween—or Happy All Hallows' Eve, I guess. It's amazing the things I've learned over the last year about your culture and the various holidays that it helps to support.

What am I doing tonight? I'm actually working, big surprise, though Mr. Husseini gave me permission to hand out candy, even giving me a couple of big bags of varieties from stock.

What's your favorite candy bar?

Mine is definitely Snickers. If you haven't had one of those yet, you're missing out.

Maybe you only know European candy?

I'd ask you what you're dressing as . . . but I already can guess which costume Edmund's required everyone to wear.

I pulled an old Santa hat out of the storage closet at the store.

Smiled at myself the whole damn time.

Too bad nobody else gets the joke like I do.

And like I know you will.

Dex

From: aidan@npenterprises.com
To: dhawkins357@illinois.chi.edu
Date: October 31, 2022, 10:48 AM

Dex—

Dressing as Sam for All Hallows' Eve, what a brilliant idea!

I love it. Wish I could see you like that in person. Wish that our stupid system let me get pictures so I could at least see it *period.*

Better believe in the next staff meeting I'm complaining about that, damn how pissed off Edmund looks.

Also, you nailed it. We're all our normal freaking selves.

North Pole elves for All Hallows' Eve.

Belinda actually argued with Edmund about this. Shocked the hell out of me.

Shocked the hell out of Edmund, too.

At the risk of sounding stupid and clueless, what's a Snickers?

Is that like a Flake? That was my favorite candy bar back in Ireland. Ronan and I would always pop into the shops on our way back to Tír na nÓg and grab a few to bribe the other elves with, if we needed them to turn a blind eye to something.

Or everything hahahaha.

Someday, hopefully soon, I'll get to try this Snickers. And maybe someday, if you're ever across the pond, you'll be able to sample a Flake.

Highly recommend.

Ten out of ten.

Gold stars all round.

Aidan

From: aidan@npenterprises.com
To: dhawkins357@illinois.chi.edu
Date: December 22, 2022, 11:52 PM

Dex,

It's two days before we leave and things have been crazy here but I just want to say one thing before the Christmas spirit overtakes everything and I don't get a chance before we see each other again.

The last twelve months exchanging emails with you has been the best damn thing that ever happened to me.

You made a hard transition so much easier.

You were a joy, and a bright light in a dark North Pole.

No matter what happens, I've been privileged to know you—and to care about you.

Because you know that's what this is. You're not just keeping me company and distracting me, you've become a lifeline. My absolute favorite person.

I don't know how I'm going to live without you after I see you again.

That's the thing that's keeping me up nights, even when I should be exhausted from a long day of work, and sleeping.

I know I'm not being cocky or confident when I say I think you feel the same way.

And that . . . makes it all so much harder, doesn't it?

Anyway, thank you for everything, but most of all, Dexter, thank you for being you.

With love,
Aidan

From: dhawkins357@illinois.chi.edu

To: aidan@npenterprises.com

Date: December 23, 2022, 6:48 AM

Aidan,

You keep talking about a light, like you don't even know the sunshine you bring to *my* life.

You're a marvel and a wonder, and on top of all of that, you're magic, too, and an elf and it breaks my mind apart every morning and every night that you want to talk to me just as much as I want to talk to you.

Just know, I'll be here. Waiting. Just for you.

Currently searching for mistletoe,
Dexter

CHAPTER FOUR

Aidan felt like his heart was going to beat out of his chest.

He and Sam had been on the sleigh for only an hour, but from the moment he'd climbed on, he'd felt like he couldn't properly take a breath. He was so excited and so nervous that he thought he might vomit.

Word vomit for sure.

He'd been thinking for months now what he would say the first moment he saw Dexter again *for real*.

There'd been about a hundred phrases he'd tried out in front of the mirror, from casual to serious to downright loving, but none of them had seemed right.

You'll know it, when it's right, Aidan had told himself. *When you get to the moment, you'll know exactly what you should say. It'll come to you, easy as breathing.*

Aidan was afraid that wasn't going to happen after all. Because they were flying closer and closer to Chicago, circling ever nearer, and the magically right words to say still seemed far away.

What if he walked into the store and he was still clueless?

What if he just gaped, speechless, at Dexter again?

All the millions of words they'd exchanged over the last three hundred and sixty-five days wouldn't make up for his silence tonight, of all nights.

"You're quiet," Sam said, as they went through Peoria. They'd just been through the suburbs and were now hitting the downtown apartment complexes, presents flying into air vents and trash chutes, magically making their way to their final destinations.

Aidan didn't think he'd ever get used to seeing it, not the way he'd gotten completely used to seeing black cauldrons overflowing with gold coins. Not the way he was used to seeing the hazy outlines of rainbows touch the edge of the horizon, between land and sky.

There was something specially magical about this.

He hadn't really paid much attention last year, too cold at first and then too distracted.

This year he wasn't *not* distracted, no way, but he almost wanted a distraction from his distraction. And Sam? He was an extraordinary one.

He'd been slowly, inevitably absorbing the love and joy the North Pole elves held for Christmas.

He'd seen it coming, known that he was enjoying the idea of it more and more, but he was still blown away by the culmination of a year's worth of study and absorption finally coming to fruition.

Or maybe that was the look on Sam's face.

He hadn't seen it last year.

Or maybe he hadn't known what it meant.

But he knew now.

It was love, condensed into its purest, most unadulterated, truly unselfish form.

It was giving, just to see the joy that receiving brought to the people of the world.

It wasn't just the toys themselves. It was the idea that someone out there cared about *them*. About every single one of them.

Aidan realized, just as they were cresting over Chicago, why all of this mattered so much to Edmund.

His angsting and his fierce attention to detail and his protectiveness of hundreds of years of North Pole tradition—that was what made tonight happen.

And Aidan, though he would probably never want to admit it, was grateful to him.

That was when he realized that if he was going to speak up, he was going to have to do it now.

"You doing alright?" Aidan asked, trying to school his expression into something casual. Not pointed. Not like he'd waited until just now to ask.

"I'm perfectly alright, my young friend," Sam said in his normally jovial voice. "Are you not alright?"

"Oh, I am. Totally alright. Just you know, wanted to double-check. See if you needed a snack. Something to eat. Maybe some milk to drink."

Sam slid him a look. "A snack?"

"Yeah," Aidan said. Praying he wasn't too transparent. He hadn't ever considered the possibility that he couldn't convince Sam to stop and to stop where they had last year.

Anything else was unthinkable.

He *had* to see Dexter again.

"You thirsty, huh, my boy?" Sam's eyes were twinkling, but there was no way he could *know*. Nobody knew.

Of course if Sam was as magical as he seemed, as everyone said he was, maybe he could sense Aidan's heart beating as hard and fast as it had beat in his whole life.

If he could sense it, he'd know that something was going on, something that wasn't quite as straightforward as Aidan's request for a snack.

But that, Aidan decided, didn't matter.

He was committed. He was in this.

He'd do whatever it took to see Dexter.

"I'm really thirsty," Aidan said, only partially lying. He was thirsty and he was hungry—but for a person, not for Oreos and not for milk. "Can we please stop?"

He'd studied the maps, not just because Edmund had insisted he do so, but because he'd really wanted to be sure of the point of no return. When he needed Sam to stop. How far away Mr. Husseini's store was from various different points in the city where Sam could land the sleigh.

"You seem awfully eager for a snack," Sam said, still twinkling like that. "But I suppose I could use some Oreos and a chocolate milk. Like last year?" His smile now, kind and understanding, like he *got* just how important this was to Aidan, blew Aidan's mind.

Because he wasn't supposed to know.

That doesn't matter now, Aidan told himself, as his heart somehow impossibly accelerated as Sam pulled the sleigh into the exact same alley he had only twelve months earlier.

"Don't be too long now," Sam said kindly.

"I won't, I really won't," Aidan said, even though he hoped that he might be *just* long enough, and then he was scrambling down off the sleigh, his heartbeat thundering in his ears.

He'd only been along this route once before, though last year he hadn't known where he was going.

This year, his feet carried him along his path like they'd walked it a hundred times, a thousand. And maybe in his head, he had.

He'd definitely spent enough time poring over the maps of this particular area, wondering which sandwich shops Dexter liked to stop at, which corners he loitered at, waiting for the light to change, which route he took between his apartment building and Mr. Husseini's shop.

And then, suddenly, there it was.

There were Christmas lights strung up around all the front windows, and the Open sign flashed merrily in the corner.

Aidan took a deep, unsteady breath and pushed the door open.

It was practically a repeat of three hundred and sixty-five days ago.

Aidan stopped in his tracks, right inside the door.

He heard it shut behind him.

Dexter was behind the counter. His hair was a little longer, but he'd shaved, and the Bah Humbug shirt was back.

He was just as attractive as he'd been the year before, except he was so much more now. Because Aidan had discovered that he wasn't just handsome on the outside, he was beautiful inside, too. That he was funny and clever and achingly kind, and God, so damn supportive.

Everything that Aidan had ever wanted in another human being.

So it made sense, in some kind of twisted way, that he opened his mouth and then shut it again, because nothing came out.

Not even something stupid and silly. But actually, nothing at all.

Dexter was still staring at him. Then he walked slowly around the corner, just as silent as Aidan himself, and then they were facing each other.

Aidan swallowed hard. Forced words into his mouth.

Words that weren't, "I'm crazy about you." Words that weren't, "Let's run away together and see how far we can get." Words that definitely weren't, "Is there a back room here? How fast do you think we can get our clothes off?"

Aidan had endured one horribly awkward conversation with Billy about sex, and if this whole thing was just about sex. "It's not," he insisted, because how could it be? They'd only vaguely referred to sex. But it wasn't *not* about sex either, because sometimes it felt like the promise of it was hidden in every space between every word they'd ever sent each other.

The words Aidan ended up with were actually one word, singular.

"Hey."

The corner of Dex's mouth quirked up and Aidan was swamped with it. He felt lightheaded.

"Hey," Dex said back. "I . . . uh . . . I got you something? You said you didn't get anything last year and . . ." He reached into his pocket and produced a slightly wrinkled package, wrapped in silver and green paper.

"Green," Dex said, rubbing the back of his neck and looking like he was terrified and excited and every other emotion in between after Aidan took the package, "because I thought you'd like that."

"I like green," Aidan said. Apparently basics were all he was capable of.

He unwrapped it, and the green and silver paper fell away to reveal a small box, which he popped open. Inside was a maroon velvet box. Like a ring box.

Aidan's fingers shook and he nearly dropped it on the floor as he tried to get it open.

A ring? Dexter had gotten him a *ring*?

But no, he popped the box open and realized it wasn't a ring at all.

It was a small coin, hung on a chain.

Aidan looked closer and realized that he recognized it. A number of years back all the countries in the EU had gone to a standarized form of coinage.

But this was from before that. When Ireland had had its own currency.

This was a very old coin. Not ancient, but old. From almost when Aidan was a very young lad, first sneaking onto the streets of Dublin with Ronan.

He plucked it out of the box, holding the chain with one finger.

"So you'd always have it with you," Dexter said softly. "Ireland, I mean. Tír na nÓg."

"I . . ." Aidan wet his hips. Swallowed. His throat was suddenly dry and tight. Dex's dark eyes were intense. So much more intense than Aidan remembered them, but then the last time they hadn't known each other.

It had just been fifteen minutes in a store on Christmas Eve.

A random encounter with possibilities, but not much more than that.

Tonight was . . .

Aidan wasn't sure he had the words yet, so instead, he slipped the chain around his neck.

"It's perfect," he said quietly. "I love it. Thank you."

Dexter's smile was perfect. It warmed up all the parts of Aidan that had been cold for all these months.

"You're welcome," he said.

Aidan bit his bottom lip. "I . . . I didn't get anything for you," he said.

"It's okay," Dex responded back immediately, "you brought yourself, that's what's important." And that was all he got out before Aidan said simply, without overthinking, just *feeling*, "All I wanted to get you was this."

The distance between them was closed in less than two steps and then he reached up and pressed his lips against Dexter's.

Dexter couldn't have been very surprised that it happened.

After all, how many times had they referenced kissing in their emails? They hadn't talked much about sex or the specifics of sex, but kissing? Oh, that came up frequently. The last email that Dexter had sent had even referenced meeting him under the mistletoe.

So, it wasn't that he was surprised.

Maybe it was the way they fit together, as flawlessly as they had in every single one of Aidan's dreams, the lushness of Dex's bottom lip against his own, moving slow as molasses, gently at first, then like he was waking up from a dream, more quickly, more forcefully.

Then they were kissing with abandon, Dexter wrapping his arms around him so tightly that Aidan wasn't sure he could breathe—though breathing was completely overrated anyway—and pulling him flush against him, mouth devouring Aidan's with a ferocity and a determination that Aidan matched kiss by kiss.

It felt like it went on forever. His heart was racing, his nerves were aching, every inch of him thrilled when Dexter ran his hands across him, over him, wanting to feel every inch of him.

And Aidan? Aidan felt him too.

Dex was a wondrous combination of soft and hard, a delicious juxtaposition of textures. His chest and stomach were firm, his cock, pressed against him was undeniably hard, but his mouth was soft and yielding, his fingertips gentle yet persistent, his hair just at the back of his neck silky, the skin underneath it, even silkier.

Aidan wanted to feel more of it. He wanted to feel all of it.

He was almost sixty-eight years old. He'd kissed elves and humans, and even memorably, one goblin, on a dare from Ronan. He'd never had a kiss like this one before, and he didn't think he ever would again.

It was the kind of kiss that could power a thousand daydreams and a hundred fantasies. No matter what happened between them, Aidan knew he would never forget it. Never forget Dex.

And then, abruptly, horribly, it ended.

Dexter was breathing hard, his mouth red and wet, his pupils huge and dark. He looked both wretched and desperate, and Aidan understood.

They had maybe, at most, a few minutes left.

That was going to have to be enough to last them God only knew how much longer.

Dex jammed his hands into the pockets of his jeans. Like he had to do it, so he wouldn't grab Aidan again.

Aidan wanted to be grabbed more than he wanted to take his next breath.

But he understood. Even if he hated it.

"I don't think that was a gift just for me," Dexter finally said, a glimmer of a smile finally emerging on his handsome face.

"No," Aidan agreed, smiling too.

Before he could stop himself, he reached out and smoothed Dex's hair back from his forehead. It was so soft, it was almost impossible to tear his hands away.

Maybe Dexter had the right idea after all.

"How much longer ..."

"Don't," Aidan begged. He hadn't wanted this to feel like a particularly sappy goodbye in one of those romantic movies that Belinda loved to watch. Hadn't wanted it to feel wrenching and sad like that. Had only wanted to bask in the joy of finally seeing Dex again.

The problem was that now that he'd seen him again, and *kissed* him, he wanted to do it all the time. Even more than he'd wanted to before.

And that was a *lot* of wanting.

He didn't feel like he could even contain it.

"Okay," Dexter said with a soft smile, like he understood.

Maybe he did. Because that was one thing they'd always done: understood each other.

It didn't make sense because Dex was a human and he was an elf, but he'd learned over the last year that the truth and logic didn't always go hand in hand.

"I should get some cookies for Sam," Aidan said.

If he returned empty-handed, that would be suspicious. He had a weird prickly feeling at the back of his neck, an elves' intuition, that Sam already suspected something.

Dexter followed him to the cookie and chip aisle, and Aidan could feel his eyes on his back, intent, as he scanned the shelves.

"Oreos," Aidan said suddenly, "are always a solid choice."

Dexter laughed then, loud and bright, and it was like the bells at the highest tower in the North Pole, the ones that rang at dawn on Christmas Day.

There weren't a *lot* of things that Aidan loved yet about the North Pole, but those bells? They were already a happy memory, and now Dex's laugh joined them.

"Oreos *are* a solid choice," Dex said, "and of course you can go with the traditional, because you know, it's Santa, I'm assuming he's pretty much a traditional guy, *or* you could try these peppermint bark ones. They're delicious."

"Sam loves peppermint bark, how'd you know that?" Aidan asked absently as he grabbed the package.

Dexter shot him a look. It hit Aidan dead on and made him hot and cold all over. It made him want to grab him by that stupid t-shirt and drag him closer, put his mouth all over Dexter's again.

But they'd already established that way led to disaster and insanity—or maybe the kind of legendary blue balls that could inspire a particularly lengthy elvish epic poem.

"He's Santa," Dexter said slowly. "You know the guy, he's like a symbolic representation of Christmas."

"I have met him before," Aidan retorted teasingly.

"Good, I thought you might have," Dexter said right back, not even waiting til Aidan's words had faded.

"Definitely the chocolate milk still," Aidan said as they headed towards the drink case at the back of the store. "He really liked that addition, by the way."

"Santa thinks I've got good taste," Dex said a little smugly. "Looks like I'm not the only one who thinks so." The way his gaze lingered on Aidan's body made it clear just what he was congratulating himself for noticing: *him.*

It warmed him up and turned him inside out.

"Can you . . ." Aidan gestured to the shelf with the milk. At the very top of the large cooler. "I can't reach."

"It shouldn't be cute," Dex mused as he pulled the door open, "but it is."

Aidan raised an eyebrow as they headed back towards the front of the store. "That I'm short?"

"You're not even that short, not the way I thought elves were supposed to be," Dexter pointed out as he went behind the counter. *Too far away*, Aidan's body screamed, *he's too far away.* Even though since the kiss they'd both done their best not to touch.

Did that make it easier?

Aidan wasn't sure.

This was hard, no matter what they seemed to do. Or not do.

"We've talked about this," Aidan said. "There's a lot of fake news about elves out there."

"I bet that drives Edmund crazy," Dex said with a little grin as he sat down on the chair behind the counter, propping his head up on his elbow. His eyes were so dark, so kind and hot and adoring, Aidan thought he could stand here forever, and just lose himself in them.

"What?" Aidan said, shaking his head a little. Trying to clear it. "Edmund? Oh, he hates it. Is always going on and on about an 'educational campaign,' until someone reminds him that it doesn't really matter what humans think of us. Might even help keep our secrets, if they don't know the truth."

"Well," Dex said, "you've no idea how flattered and honored I am to be one of the few that does."

"How do you know you're not the *only* one?" Aidan teased.

"How about this," Dexter said in a sweet drawl, "I like to think I'm not the only human out there who's ever been charmed by an elf. Maybe you're not the only elf who's managed to charm one. Maybe we're not the only star-crossed lovers out there."

Aidan swallowed hard at the word, "lovers," coming out of Dex's mouth. He wanted to taste the way that word felt, on Dex's tongue.

"Ah, well, maybe not," Aidan said.

He knew he needed to go.

Sam would be waiting.

Any longer and Sam's suspicions might bloom into something else. If that happened, then there was no telling what he'd do. He might even tell Edmund, and then hell would break loose.

But Aidan would not be lying if he said it was going to just about kill him to walk out the door, not knowing if he'd see Dex in a few months or a few weeks or in another three hundred and sixty-five days.

"Hey," Dex said, "I forgot your other present."

Oh yes, please kiss me again, Aidan thought.

But instead of coming around the counter, Dexter whipped something out from under the counter. "Snickers," he said, setting the candy bar alongside the package of Oreos and the chocolate milk. "Even elves could use a pick-me-up on Christmas Eve."

For a long second, Aidan stared at the candy bar on the counter. It was just one thing that they'd talked about out of a thousand, but Dexter had remembered.

Had *cared.*

He must have looked a whole bunch of ways, because suddenly, Dex was walking around the edge of the counter and Aidan was in his arms again, and their second kiss blew even the first one away.

How had he ever thought he could turn his back on this?

Touching Dex was like breathing, his fingers curling into his t-shirt, wanting to delve into his skin.

He never wanted to leave him.

Their mouths moved together like this kiss had been choreographed in advance, like they already *knew* each other, but their bodies were just now catching up.

And then suddenly, a noise broke through.

Was it Dexter panting?

Was it him?

Aidan didn't really care, but then it happened again, and again.

He felt Dex's grip tighten on him, and then he realized what that sound was.

It was someone clearing their throat.

Aidan took his mouth off Dexter's, even though he felt the loss of it almost immediately, and turned.

It wasn't just any someone.

It was Sam.

Santa.

And the expression on his face wasn't upset or shocked or even angry.

It was undeniably amused. It was *delighted*.

Aidan swallowed hard.

"Thought I told you to try to make it quick," Sam said, brushing a bit of lint off his red velvet tunic. His eyes twinkled. "Understand why you don't want to, but we've got to get going. Lots of presents to deliver."

"Right."

Aidan was afraid to even look back to Dexter. Was sure he already knew what he'd look like. Torn between an understandable awe and also likely embarrassment at being caught making out by Santa himself.

It was even worse than being caught by your dad.

"You'd better go," Dexter said quietly, apparently recovering his wits.

"I . . ." Aidan couldn't resist a second longer and turned to look at Dex.

There was anguish and embarrassment and maybe something that might have been love, all warring in his face, and in his eyes.

"I'll be at the sleigh," Sam said kindly. "Oh, are these our snacks?"

"Yes," Dexter said, not even bothering to look at Sam.

"Thank you kindly. Be quick about it, Aidan."

The door shut behind Sam.

"I guess . . ." Dexter swallowed hard. Aidan watched as his Adam's apple bobbed. "I guess you'd better go."

"Thank you for the necklace. Thank you for . . ." Aidan was thankful, was downright fucking grateful for everything Dex was. How could he even say it? There weren't words for what he was feeling.

The highs, and the inevitable lows.

"I know," Dex said and then he was tugging him into a tight, warm embrace. Holding him so close that for a second, Aidan imagined that they could do this all the time.

"I . . ." Aidan felt his voice dying. He couldn't say it. Not like this. Not when they were saying goodbye.

Dexter squeezed him even tighter.

"I know that too," Dexter said.

And then somehow, Aidan let him go, turned and walked away.

Chapter Five

Aidan wasn't proud of it, but he dragged his feet all the way back to where the sleigh was parked. He *was* proud that he didn't turn tail and just run back to the store, back into Dex's arms.

Maybe later, when the presents had been delivered, and they'd returned to the North Pole, when he finally got a moment to himself, he might shed a few tears over having to leave him again.

But for now, there was a job to do.

When he climbed into the sleigh, there was a dusting of chocolate crumbs across Sam's long, white beard.

"I know it would be hard to leave him, Aidan," Sam said kindly. "So I appreciate you doing it."

"How do you know anything about it?" Aidan asked, a little grumpy, because well, he'd *had* to leave him and it hurt like hell.

Sam's smile was grave. "I know more than you realize."

"Oh." Aidan hesitated. "You haven't told Edmund, right?"

"Do you want me to tell Edmund about it?"

"No, no, no, definitely not, he'll freak out, he'll . . ." Aidan trailed off. "You know what he'll do."

"Yes, it's likely he wouldn't understand," Sam agreed with a solemn nod. "Besides, what kind of Christmas spirit would I be promoting if I didn't give you what you wanted the most?"

"Not a very good Santa," Aidan admitted.

"Well, then, now that we've settled that," Sam said, "we'd better get back on the road. Lots of gifts left to deliver."

"Right," Aidan said. He could already imagine the email he would write to Dex when they finally got back to the North Pole.

He wasn't even going to wait til the new year.

Also, if Sam had known and had let him come anyway . . . he might be willing to smooth Dex's way to moving to the North Pole.

It was that thought that kept his attitude positive as Sam went through the liftoff procedure, flicking switches and hitting buttons, and right as they were about to rise off the ground, the engine gave a sputter and then expelled a load of foul-smelling smoke and then clattered to an abrupt stop.

"Uh-oh," Sam said. He looked concerned.

Aidan recognized that concern, because it was building inside him, sickly and rotten, making him feel ill.

"What's wrong with it?" Aidan asked.

Sam shot him a look. "Aren't you supposed to know that?" he asked.

Technically true.

One of the reasons an elf always accompanied Santa was because they had the technical know-how in case the sleigh broke down.

Supposed to being the key part of the phrase here, because while Aidan had studied the diagrams of the engine and the thingamajig that helped give the sleigh lift and flight, he wasn't nearly at the point where he could understand them.

Nevermind apply his minuscule knowledge to the problem and fix it.

"Uh," Aidan said, hedging. "Technically yes. In reality, not really so much."

Sam sighed. "I guess when they foretold the Elf Who Would Save Christmas, they didn't expect that he'd have to be mechanically inclined."

"It would've made more sense," Aidan agreed.

"Well, how are we going to handle this? Do you want to take a look?"

"I can," Aidan agreed. "But I don't want . . . just setting expectations."

Sam looked at him blankly. "But we can't deliver presents without the sleigh."

"Really? From what I understand, you could sit here, and never move and use your magic to deliver the presents to every child on this planet."

Sam chuckled under his breath. "Because that's what I'm already doing, right?"

"Yeah, I mean, we land someplace near, often on a roof, and you do an entire neighborhood," Aidan said. "I tried to tell Edmund once that you never needed to leave the North Pole."

"There's a certain magic in tradition," Sam said heavily. "And also, the further the distance, the larger the strain is on my magic. So while I could do the whole of Chicago and its suburbs from this spot, any further and well, I'd likely tap out. Have nothing left for the rest of the trip."

Aidan leaned back against the seat. "Shit," he said. "So we have to fix the sleigh."

Sam raised an eyebrow. "You're supposed to be the sleigh fixer in this partnership."

"Guess I'll take a look," Aidan said. "Maybe it'll be easy. Maybe it'll come to me. After all, I'm supposedly the Christmas Savior, right?"

"You're not supposedly the Savior, Aidan," Sam said, giving him a reassuring pat on the shoulder. "You *are* the Savior. That's how I know you'll figure something out."

"Bet you're missing the reindeer right about now," Aidan said as he climbed down out of the sleigh. Found the latch that kept the shiny red lacquered hood closed. Released it, and to his relief, the hood lifted, revealing all the magical and mechanical devices that powered the sleigh and gave it the ability to fly at record speeds around the world.

The problem was that while he *had* studied the diagrams, trying to understand how all these systems worked together, he'd never made it past a rudimentary understanding. Because, just like Sam had said, he wasn't gifted at this kind of thing.

He was good at logistics.

Organizing people and products and events.

Analyzing data.

Not troubleshooting engines.

Just start at the beginning, Aidan told himself, *and stay calm. As soon as you freak out, your brain's gonna shut down.*

Mentally pulling up the most basic diagram he'd studied, he started to recognize a few of the main systems. That there, with the red tubes, that was the main engine. The other thing, with the blue and the silver, that was the flying mechanism. And the green box on the far left, that was the magical power that helped them achieve the height and the speed that made it possible for Sam to deliver so many presents.

Smoke was currently billowing from all three.

Damnit, Aidan swore under his breath.

"Any luck?" Sam asked hopefully.

Aidan stared at the black smoke spewing from the engine, at the silver-gray steam coming from the flying mechanism. And the ugly purple glittery cloud rising above the magical doohickey.

"Working on it," Aidan said, trying to fake bravado and confidence that he didn't feel.

Almost unbidden, Dex's face came to mind.

He'd encouraged him, over the last year, to study this stuff harder, to ask more questions, but Aidan had blown it off. Had never imagined that he might actually *need* any of it.

What if instead of being the Elf Who Saved Christmas, he ended up being the elf who ruined the entire goddamn holiday?

If they had to rely on Aidan's knowledge and ability to fix the sleigh, they'd never get it done, but if . . . Aidan thought of Dexter again.

He'd never seen a single diagram but he was a gifted mechanical engineer. He'd worked on engines, and lots of different kinds of gadgets. He was extremely good at fixing things.

He'd fixed Mr. Husseini's toaster oven just last week.

Maybe . . . just maybe he could come over here and help Aidan fix the sleigh.

"Sam," Aidan said cautiously, "*Santa*, what if . . . what if I'm not the one who's meant to fix it?"

Sam glanced up from the control panel. "What do you mean? I'm certainly not capable of figuring it out."

"Dex . . . Dexter, the guy at the store, my friend, he's really good at this kind of thing. He's about to graduate with a master's in mechanical engineering. He fixes things all the time."

"But he doesn't know anything about the sleigh. Or about magic."

"But I do," Aidan argued, more than a little desperate.

Not just because he was already dying to see Dex again.

"So you're suggesting you go find him again and bring him here, to help you fix the sleigh," Sam said neutrally.

"I'm honestly afraid that all I'd do is end up breaking it worse," Aidan confessed. "I know just enough to be dangerous."

"But this Dexter, as much as you like him, Aidan, and I know you do, he knows even less."

"Yeah, but he's *good* at this," Aidan said. "I hate to say it so bluntly, but your vaunted Christmas Savior, well, he's shit at anything like this. Give me something to organize. The presents, maybe, or the next Christmas Gala, or even let me analyze the data from years past, but this? I'm unsuited to it, and I haven't had nearly enough time to pick it up."

Sam looked stern. "This isn't just an excuse to see him again, is it?"

"No," Aidan said, and it wasn't a lie. "I'll be honest. I do want to see him again, desperately, but I also know how important this is. Children all over the world are waiting for their gifts—and it isn't just the gifts, is it? It's that you care. That you made the effort. For so many of these children, nobody else cares."

Sam's expression softened. "You understand."

"I don't want to be the one to let them down," Aidan said. Realized that he was begging. Pleading. To be allowed to do the one thing that might actually be enough to save them. He *was* the Christmas Savior wasn't he?

"Then you won't," Sam said firmly. "Go get Dexter. See if he can help us."

Dexter could still taste Aidan when he licked his lower lip.

Could still feel the pressure and the weight of him in his arms.

It had been the best fifteen minutes of his life, and the worst, too.

Because it had begun, and then it had ended.

He'd known that it would. That much he'd come to terms with before Aidan had ever arrived. Long before the holiday season had even begun.

Before they'd even put out the Christmas lights and the inflatable gnomes and teddy bears and life-size Santa Clauses at Target.

But it had hit him totally different than how he'd thought it would. He hadn't been prepared for the way the pain wouldn't just ache, but would tear, with claws and purpose, leaving him feeling ripped apart.

What were you supposed to do when you found the guy of your dreams and he wasn't even a human like you?

Dex didn't know.

But he was going to have to figure it out.

He'd been sitting there, trying not to feel the sheer loneliness crowd onto him, now that Aidan had arrived and then left, trying to think of a way out of their predicament, ever since Aidan had walked out the door.

He hadn't made it all that far when the front door to the store opened again.

Dex's head popped up and he told himself, very firmly, not to get his hopes up. Aidan was gone. He was assisting Santa. His job was important as hell. Even someone who thought Christmas was mostly materialistic bullshit couldn't come face-to-face with Santa and not have a few of his opinions rocked.

But he'd already come to terms with the fact that Aidan wouldn't be back for another year.

Three hundred and sixty-five more days.

And yet, Dex could barely believe his own eyes because that was Aidan's hair, wasn't it? Bright as a gold coin. And his eyes, an impossibly light green, and his adorable, beloved face. Except that he wasn't smiling. Not like he had when he'd walked in before.

"Dex," Aidan said, coming to stand in front of the counter, "I'm afraid we need some help."

"Is everything okay?" Dex was already coming out from behind the counter, and only the concern in Aidan's expression kept him from reaching for the elf again.

It was like he was addicted to touching him. Maybe because for all those days in between, he couldn't.

"No, it's not okay. The sleigh is . . . well, it's not working. It broke down. Won't start. Won't fly. Lots of smoke," Aidan said, waving his arms around. Apparently illustrating the smoke. Dex held back his smile because he was adorably charming even when he wasn't trying to be.

"You need to use the phone?"

Dex had already learned the hard way that elves didn't carry phones. There were no long phone calls, no texting, definitely no FaceTiming. Dex had to admit he was a little bitter about that.

"Who are we gonna call? The North Pole?" Aidan shook his head and then wrapped a hand around Dexter's forearm. "No, I need *your* help."

"Wait," Dexter said, as Aidan began to tug him. "You want *me* to fix the sleigh?"

Aidan nodded emphatically. "That's what I've been trying to say."

"I'm not sure what help I can be," Dex said hesitantly. "You're the one who's studied the diagrams."

Aidan shot him a look that made Dex want to push him up against the counter and kiss him silly. "You know I'm not good at this. And you are."

"Santa is okay with this?"

"He's not *not* okay with it," Aidan said. "We need to get the sleigh fixed and if we rely on my knowledge..."

"Okay," Dexter said, not quite believing he was agreeing to this. "I can't make any promises, but you know the rudimentary ideas behind the mechanics, and maybe that's enough to help me diagnose the problem."

"And fix it."

Dexter ran a hand through his hair. "Yeah, let's not get ahead of ourselves. I'll have to text Mr. Husseini, let him know I'm closing the store early..."

"Then text him," Aidan said. He was bossier than Dex had imagined when they'd first met. He'd gotten hints of it, little tastes of it, over the course of a year's worth of emails, but then Aidan had still been adjusting to a new environment, so he hadn't been quite himself.

But Dex thought he might be seeing the real Aidan right now, and just like every other part of the man, he was head over heels crazy about this personality trait, too.

There wasn't anything about Aidan that Dex wasn't crazy about.

Except the part where he lived three hundred and sixty-four days a year in the North Pole.

"Okay, okay, give me a second," Dexter grumbled. He grabbed his phone and sent a quick text to Mr. Husseini, letting him know he was closing the store early tonight because a friend was having an emergency. He'd assume the friend was Jonathan, and that was okay. Also, Mr. Husseini wouldn't even be upset about the lost revenue, because he'd actually tried not to open this year on Christmas Eve, or even to close early, but Dexter had insisted on being there and taking the shift.

He'd had to be here for Aidan.

Mr. Husseini, if he ever found out the truth, would be happy for him. Like Jonathan, he was disappointed that Dexter didn't have anyone in his life.

"You done?" Aidan asked impatiently as Dexter counted the cash and stuck the tiny amount the store had made tonight into the safe, locking it up tight.

"Yeah, let me just grab my coat and lock the front door. I'll meet you around front," Dexter said. "It's easier if I go through the back."

"The back?" Aidan asked speculatively. "Can I come with you instead?"

Dex didn't know why he'd want to, but he also wasn't going to turn down more time with Aidan.

That would be counter to every single damn thing he wanted.

"Sure, I don't see why not," Dex said, locking the front door with his set of keys, and then flicking the switch that powered the "Open" sign on the front window.

Aidan followed him when he pushed open the door that led to the back storeroom.

Dexter did a quick once-over, made sure everything was in its place and was about to set the alarm and then flick the lights off, when suddenly his arms were full of Aidan again.

It was unexpected, but it wasn't a bad kind of surprise.

Actually, it was the best kind of surprise.

Dex staggered back half a step, and then kissed Aidan back, everything in him heating up instantly like he'd never had to let Aidan go.

Dexter wasn't nearly done with him when Aidan pulled away, grinning, his breath coming in short pants. "I wondered," he said.

"If you'd like kissing me?"

"No," Aidan said, laughing. "I knew I'd love kissing you. That wasn't even up for debate. I wondered when I was here before, if you had a back room where we could be . . . well, *alone*, and you do."

"Is the sleigh really broken down or were you just trying to lure me back here?" Dex teased.

"Unfortunately, it's really broken down," Aidan said. "But I got another kiss out of it. Can't be too sad about that."

Dexter's fingers were still trembling a bit when he punched in the alarm code. "I'm not sad either. Not even a little. Maybe if we can't fix the sleigh . . ."

"Don't think like that," Aidan said, tucking his fingers into Dexter's, squeezing tightly. "You can do anything."

When Aidan talked like that, Dexter thought that maybe he could.

He flicked the light switch off and let the back door close behind them.

"Wait," Dex said as they turned the corner around the building, "I don't have any of my tools."

"It's okay, there's a tool kit on the sleigh. Probably a little different than you're used to, but it should work just fine."

"North Pole tools, and I'm working on Santa's sleigh." Dex heard the thread of hysteria in his voice. "I guess I can't complain about a lack of imagination anymore, can I?"

"Guess not," Aidan said, and the look he shot Dex was impudent and adorable.

Dexter wanted to kiss it off of him.

If Aidan was like any other guy, and if Santa himself—and an entire world of children—weren't waiting on them, he might have. But one of the reasons he'd gone into this line of work was because solving problems, especially problems that had everyone else stumped, where the solution could make a real difference, was incredibly gratifying.

He'd done small things, on a small scale. Fixing Mr. Husseini's toaster oven. Figuring out that Jonathan's transmission didn't need to be rebuilt after all. But this was a totally different kind of pressure.

As they finally reached the mouth of the alley and Dexter saw the shiny red sleigh for the first time, just as Aidan had described it to him, he found his excitement beginning to overtake his apprehension.

"It's beautiful, isn't it?" Aidan asked as they approached.

But Dex had already left the flawless lacquered exterior behind, drawn like a moth to a flame to the open hood, with its mysterious, magical components exposed.

Though the harder he looked, the more he recognized.

That was the engine there. He could identify most of the components and their functions, easily.

"What's this?" he asked Aidan, pointing to the blue and silver embellished box. "Exhaust? Catalytic converter?"

"It's the flight mechanism," Aidan said, peering closer. He nudged Dex with his shoulder. "Tools," he said, pointing down to a matching shiny red tool kit. Aidan touched the top of the carrying case and it suddenly multiplied, going from a single level to seven, like it was magic.

It is magic, Dex thought, gawking at how what had looked like a rudimentary portable kit had expanded into a full tool chest. "Here's how you work the drawers," Aidan said, giving the front panel of one a single touch, and the drawer opened on its own in a smooth motion. Dexter caught a glimpse of perfect, shiny silver tools all laid out in neat rows before Aidan pushed it closed with another touch of his finger.

"Hydraulics?" Dex asked, even though he already knew the answer.

Aidan shook his head. "Well, *maybe* initially," he said, "but magic, too."

"Nothing is going to turn my hands green or make me grow a second head, right?" Dex asked, with a nervous laugh. Before last Christmas, he hadn't given one thought to magic, and if it was real or not.

Now it was rapidly becoming part of his life.

"Of course not," Aidan said. "And I'll be right here. I might not know enough to diagnose and fix the problem, but I know some of how the magic works."

"Aidan sells himself a bit short."

Dexter glanced up and there was Santa.

It was going to be difficult to ever get used to that.

He'd seen those websites and blogs, with their "Santa lookalike pics," but Santa—or Sam, as Aidan called him—was the essence and the distillation of everything that popular culture wanted in a Santa figure.

At first, Dexter hadn't been able to figure out what it was that really brought *this* Santa to full Santa-esque life, but as he looked at him now, he realized it was the kindness in his eyes.

"I believe that, sir," Dexter agreed.

Santa threw his head back and laughed. "Well, I haven't been called that in a very long time. Call me Sam. I just wanted to check in and make sure that Aidan got you everything you needed."

"Oh, absolutely, this kit is well, it's way better than my regular tools." He'd cobbled them together from several different sets, over the years, and while he loved his tool kit, it was nothing like this one, everything new and shiny and perfect —and *magical*.

"Good," Sam said with an approving nod. "I'm going to leave you two to figure out the problem."

"You're going to leave?" Aidan sounded apprehensive.

"I can get some of the suburbs done on foot," Sam said, patting Aidan on the shoulder. "Don't worry about me, I'll be just fine."

"Are you sure you don't want me to come with you?"

Dex could hear the undercurrent of fear in Aidan's voice. Probably he was worried what Edmund's reaction would be if something happened to Sam. Or if Edmund discovered that he'd let him go off on his own.

"Of course not," Sam scoffed. "You have plenty to do here, to help Dexter get the sleigh up and running. By the time I return . . ."

"It will be," Aidan promised, even though Dexter wouldn't have been quite so eager to make that particular vow.

"Excellent. Good luck," Sam said, and then pulling his fur-lined red hood over his head, took off towards the entry of the alley.

"I guess," Aidan said with trepidation as Sam disappeared around the corner, "I guess we're on our own now."

Chapter Six

"And what's this?" Dex asked. He'd taken his jacket off, even though it was cold in the alley, and pushed up the sleeves of the henley he was wearing underneath his "Bah Humbug" t-shirt. Aidan didn't want to be distracted by the lean muscles of his forearms, but he supposed it was probably inevitable.

"That's the magical power source," Aidan said, following where Dexter was pointing.

"Any chance that's the problem?" Dex asked.

He'd suggested that they go through each component in the sleigh, trying to narrow down exactly what the problem was, before they could attempt a fix.

In the last ten minutes, Aidan had wished more than once that he'd paid more attention to Edmund's diagrams than he had daydreaming about the man next to him.

But at least Aidan knew this much. "No," he said, "it's still glowing bright white. If the magic wasn't working or if it was corrupted, it wouldn't look like that anymore. It'd be dull and dingy."

"Okay." Dex sounded frustrated.

"What's wrong?"

"Well, I was hoping it was going to be something easy, maybe even something quick, like a loose hose or a disconnected cable, but . . ." Dex sighed. "It looks like it might be more serious than that. I was also hoping I could get by without actually dismantling any of the components, because it's always a risk to take stuff apart if you don't understand it. What if I put it back together wrong and create more problems? But I'm not sure we have a choice."

Aidan looked at the open compartment, and then back up at Dex.

"I wouldn't have asked you to help if I didn't think you weren't equal to the task," Aidan said. "Where do you want to start?"

"The thing I know the most about," Dex said wryly. "The engine."

Watching Dexter work was like listening to poetry or watching a master sculptor at work. There was a purpose and a fluidity to everything he did. His fingers always plucked the right tool out of the chest, and he worked carefully but efficiently, loosening bolts with a grace that Aidan knew he'd never be able to match.

Aidan had been pretty damn sure that he'd been falling in love before, before he'd ever seen Dex again, before the kiss that had blown his world apart, before they'd ever spent more time together.

But now? Love felt like an inevitability.

There was the look in Dex's eyes as he'd glance up from his work every so often, the heat blurring the focus in them, the affection and the warmth making Aidan think of crazy things like *moving,* and *commitment,* and *forever.*

It was too soon to say something to Dex, but it was right there, on the tip of his tongue.

And if he and Dexter actually pulled this off—fixed the sleigh and saved Christmas?—then Aidan wondered if there was anything he couldn't legitimately ask for.

Including inviting his man to be by his side.

Because there was no way Dexter wasn't *his*.

"Okay, I think I'm just about ready to take this engine cover off," Dex said, nudging Aidan with an elbow.

"Oh, yeah, okay."

Dex shot him a look.

Aidan smiled back, a little embarrassed around the edges. "How do we do that again?"

"We lift," Dexter teased. "Just like this." He hooked two fingers under the side of the enameled red cover and lifted it slightly. "You just need to take your side, we'll get this off, and then I can see what's really going on inside."

"Alright," Aidan said.

Dexter counted off *one . . . two . . . three . . .* and then they lifted the cover off together, exposing the inner workings of the engine. They set the cover down on the ground, next to the sleigh, and then Dexter leaned in closer, Aidan following him, taking a careful look at the parts.

"This, here, is where the magical energy comes in," Aidan said, pointing to a clear tube, but instead of it glowing as it should—glowing like it did at the source—the tube was gray and dingy looking, like the engine wasn't getting the power it needed. And if the engine wasn't getting the power, that would explain why the other components, especially the flying mechanism, weren't working the way they should.

"Yeah, this doesn't look right," Dex said, following the tube with one finger. "Look, here's where it comes out of the magical glowy cube, and here's where it changes, like halfway to the engine compartment. Just . . . abruptly. Does that make sense to you?"

"No," Aidan said, watching as Dexter pulled back, confusion in his expression. "But then, a lot of this doesn't make sense to me."

"You're doing it again," Dexter said.

"Doing what?"

"Giving yourself very little credit," Dexter said, a glimmer of a smile on his handsome face. He rubbed his jaw. "Yeah, you're not an engineer. But you're not *bad* at this. You've studied the diagrams and the plans. When I asked a question, you had an answer every single time."

"Yeah, but sometimes I was just guessing," Aidan admitted.

"I mean," Dexter said, reaching out and tugging Aidan close, his heartbeat accelerating the nearer they grew, "you're the Christmas Savior. That means something."

"I didn't think you'd buy into that," Aidan said flippantly. "All that magical bullshit. Especially the fated, born-under-the-right-kind-of-star stuff."

But Dex's expression and his dark eyes were impossibly serious. "It's hard to think it's bullshit when I'm standing next to an engine powered by magic, that helps make it possible for Santa's sleigh to deliver presents to children all over the world," he said. "And as for it being bullshit that you're the Elf Who Will Save Christmas . . . whether you're magical and special to everyone else or not, I know that you're absolutely magical and special to me."

Unlike everyone else, Dex seemed to always see the real *him*, so this speech couldn't be anything else but the truth. He trembled, reaching up and pressing a hot kiss against Dexter's mouth.

Dex's arm tightened around him, and for a split second, their motivation for fixing anything seemed to waver.

It would be so easy to get lost in the beautiful give-and-take of the kiss. In the way that Dexter's body felt against his own.

If Santa came back and the sleigh wasn't fixed, maybe it wouldn't be the end of the world. Maybe they could figure out how to commandeer a private jet. Ride around the world in style as Santa delivered gifts.

That version of the holiday had a hazy, perfect quality to it. Aidan could even see it, in his head, him sitting on Dex's lap, trading lazy kisses, as they set the plane on autopilot and let Sam do his magical thing.

Dex breaking away with a muted gasp was like a bucketful of icy water on all the dreams in his head.

"We need to focus," Dex said. He was breathing hard. His pupils were dilated, even darker than usual, and there was a hunger in them that Aidan recognized in himself.

But Dexter still pulled back another inch and then another. "You're just really distracting," he said after a long, tense moment. "Way too distracting."

"And you're not?" Aidan said. "Put your damn coat back on, so I can stop fantasizing about your forearms, please."

"What we need," Dex said, "is to figure out why in this particular spot the magic stops . . . what does magic do when it stops working?"

"Uh, becomes corrupted? Not as powerful?" Aidan guessed.

"Okay, either of those two things is happening." Dexter reached in and squeezed the tube right where the magic seemed to fade. "Everything seems normal. Maybe we should open up the magical-power-source thing."

"You really think so?" Aidan could hear the apprehension in his own voice. He knew the least about the magical power source, mostly because that was a pretty-well-guarded secret kept by a group of North Pole elves whose whole job was to design and improve the sleigh's systems.

"Did you ever study it?" Dex asked, frowning.

"Not really, not in detail," Aidan admitted. "They didn't want to give me access to those plans. Edmund was making noise about letting me see them next year. After I'd proved myself."

"Like you haven't already proved yourself," Dexter grumbled under his breath.

"Thanks," Aidan said, putting a hand on Dex's back. It wasn't an entirely unselfish act. He loved feeling the play of his lean muscles under just two thin layers of cotton. What he *really* wanted was to feel Dex's skin, to just slide his fingertips underneath the hem of his shirt and revel in the feel of it.

But that would definitely not help fix the sleigh.

"So, what you're saying is that we should avoid this, if we can. Last possible option," Dex said.

"Yep," Aidan said. "I wouldn't touch it if I were you. I mean, you wouldn't get like a second head or green hands or anything. But a blast of that strong of elvish magic? I can't tell you what it might do to a human man."

"Great," Dex grumbled. "Any other bright ideas?"

"What about this hose, it literally changes *inside* it?"

"You think there's a blockage?"

"Or something like that," Aidan said thoughtfully. "Hard to know if we don't get into it."

"And how do we do that without getting magic everywhere? You just said you didn't know what it would do to me."

"But it's not going to do anything to *me*," Aidan said, hoping that what he remembered was true.

"So you're just going to . . . cut it? How do we get it back together?" Dexter's brows were knit together in deep thought. "What if we disconnected it from the engine, then we stick a tool down inside it, feel around and see if there's any blockages? Any reason why the magic's not working right?"

"I could do that," Aidan said. "That way if we figure out the problem, we can always put it back together, and *voila*, working engine and working sleigh, again."

"Exactly," Dex said with some satisfaction. "Okay, now to figure out how to get this hose off. . . I'll get it most of the way and then you'll have to take over, okay?"

"Here," Aidan said, reaching into the sleigh and pulling out his gloves. He'd taken them off, specifically, when they'd reached Chicago, not because it wasn't cold, because it was (though it was *nothing* compared to the North Pole), but because he'd been determined to feel as much of Dexter as he could with his bare hands.

"Gloves, good idea," Dexter said, pulling them on. They were a tight-ish fit, but they did fit, and if any extra magic leaked out while Dex was loosening the hose, it wouldn't hurt him.

If that was even what magic did to humans.

Even if elves somewhere had tested it, they certainly hadn't made their results public.

"Yeah," Aidan said, "better to be safe than sorry."

Dexter leaned in closer, examining where the hose went into the engine, and then turned to the tool chest, opening one drawer and then another, then going back to the first drawer.

"I really don't know what the best tool is to use," Dexter admitted finally. "But I guess I'll try this."

"You guess?"

"Hey, I've never seen this kind of connection before," Dexter teased, shooting Aidan a bright smile. "I'm doing the best with what I've got."

The one thing Dexter didn't like about such shiny, new tools was how slippery they were. It hadn't been so bad when he'd been using them with his bare hands, but now that he was wearing Aidan's reindeer gloves, knit in a riotous combination of red and green and gold, they kept slipping on the wool and he couldn't get the grip he needed.

"You doing okay?" Aidan asked worriedly, leaning in closer as Dex felt the wrench slip again, just when he'd finally thought he'd got ahold of it.

"Ugh, yeah, these gloves . . ." Dex said.

Aidan's smile drooped. "You don't like them? Belinda knit them for me specially. She said even though we didn't have reindeer pulling the sleigh anymore, they should still be represented. That's the kind of person she is. Always thinking about other people."

"They're very *you*, and I'm not surprised Belinda wanted you to have the reindeer with you," Dexter explained, "but they're not work gloves. There's no grip."

"Ah," Aidan said, humming a little to himself. "I get it."

"My hands just keep slipping, I'm thinking I should . . ."

"No," Aidan yelped, closing his fingers around Dex's hands, just when he'd been about to take them off. "You can't. I don't . . . I don't know what the magic will do to you."

"You don't know?" That was not reassuring.

Aidan shook his head. "It could be nothing. It could be fine. But I don't know, and I don't think you should risk it."

"I can't believe nobody knows what your magic does to humans."

Aidan shot him a look. "It sure guarantees that we don't mix, doesn't it?"

Dex nodded slowly. "Okay, well, I think you're going to have to be the one to take this bolt off, then."

He handed Aidan the wrench. "Me?" Aidan squeaked adorably. "I don't think . . ."

"Selling yourself short again," Dex reminded him with an encouraging smile. "You can do this."

"I'd feel a lot better if you did it," Aidan grumbled, "but I get it . . . we can't risk you doing it without some kind of protection."

Dex watched as he maneuvered the wrench into the engine compartment, setting the tool at the right angle and then he began to carefully twist it, trying to loosen the bolt that kept the hose in place.

"It's not budging," Aidan complained as he strained, clearly trying to get enough torque to loosen it.

"Keep trying," Dex said as he shed the gloves. He might have to risk the magic exposure, after all. If they couldn't get this loose . . . well, he didn't want to have to be the one to tell Santa that they'd failed.

"I . . . am . . . *trying*," Aidan huffed as he strained, pulling the wrench with all his strength. "It's fucking stuck."

"Here, let me try," Dexter said, reaching in and putting his hands over Aidan's. It wasn't perfect, and if something terrible happened—like the magic exploding all over, then it wouldn't be enough to protect him—but in the course of his engineering career, he'd never been particularly risk-averse.

He'd committed to whatever was needed to get the job done.

And he wasn't about to change that now, not when Aidan and Santa needed his help.

"Dex, no," Aidan said, worry seeping into his voice. He glanced back, at Dex, and the emotion in his green eyes wasn't a surprise, necessarily, but made him even more determined.

"We've got to get this loose," Dex said firmly. "Let's try to pull the wrench together."

Aidan shot him one more worried look, and Dex shifted, moving an arm around the other man, covering Aidan's hands with his own again.

"Come on," Dex said, "one or two more good twists and it'll be good."

"You seem awfully confident."

He wasn't, but he wasn't about to say that to Aidan, who thought he could do whatever he set his mind to, including but probably not restricted to, repairing Santa's magical sleigh.

"On *three*," Dex said and Aidan gave a little nod of his head.

He counted it off, and then strained, hoping one big burst of strength would loosen the bolt.

But it didn't fucking move.

"Argh," Aidan cried.

"Again," Dex said inexorably. If they didn't get this loose . . . well, he couldn't even think like that.

He counted off again, and this time Dex didn't hold back his strength. He had, before, worried that he might hurt Aidan, and that was the last thing he wanted. But they also *had* to get this bolt off.

This time, he felt it shift, and Aidan strained against him, Dex feeling every one of his muscles flexing.

It wasn't the worst time to get an erection—but it wasn't exactly a great time either.

"Is that . . ." Aidan trailed off, and Dex coughed, feeling more than a little embarrassed.

"Uh, yeah," Dex said. "Sorry." It was one thing to get hard when Aidan was in his arms and they were kissing, and Aidan's mouth felt so goddamned good against his own, but right now? All they were doing was touching.

"Don't apologize," Aidan said with a little snicker. "I think we've almost got it."

Dexter thanked whatever deities were out there watching. Maybe even Sam was, monitoring their progress from a distance. Maybe he'd even given them the extra magical boost they needed.

"One more," Dex said between clenched teeth.

His head was fucking swimming with the way Aidan smelled and felt and *was*. It was a problem. Mostly because he didn't know if he'd get him alone today—or ever.

Maybe this would be the only time Aidan would be pressed against him.

It was possible that it was that extra fillip of sexual frustration with no end in sight that wrenched the bolt loose. Whatever the cause, the bolt suddenly gave the whole way, and Aidan gasped as strands of glowing magic shot into the air and landed on their skin, right where Dex's hands were covering Aidan's.

"Shit," Dex said. It didn't burn though, didn't hurt at all. In fact . . . was it just him or were the filaments of magic touching him glowing even brighter than the ones touching Aidan?

That didn't make sense, because Aidan was the magical one —but nope, definitely it was brighter on him.

"Are you okay?" Aidan asked worriedly.

"I'm fine," Dex said, taking a step back and letting the strand, which felt fairly liquid but was also somehow contained in a fiber-like structure, drip from one hand to the other. "I don't feel any different. I don't think it affected me at all, but . .

. well, the only change seems to be that I'm making it glow brighter."

"It does seem to be brighter," Aidan agreed. "And getting even brighter."

Aidan wasn't wrong. With every passing second, the magic glowed more intensely, blazing so brilliantly that it became impossible to even look directly at it.

Finally, Dexter let it fall to the ground, and to his surprise, it sizzled when it met the icy ground, melting through several layers of packed snow, right down to the asphalt.

"That was not what I expected," Aidan remarked.

"It could've been a hell of a lot worse," Dexter agreed, and he turned back to the engine compartment. "Now, let's see what's going on with this hose."

Now that he wasn't worried about the magic affecting him negatively, he picked it up, sliding a long thin tool down its length. And just like he'd expected, he discovered a blockage.

"What's this?" he asked Aidan, using the tool to maneuver the object out of the hose, dropping it onto his hand.

It was a pebble, worn smooth.

Dex ran a thumb over it, scraping off some of the extra glowy magic, and to his shock, revealed an even more brilliant shine.

"That's a diamond," Aidan said, equally as shocked. "From the plains of the North Pole. How did that get in there?"

"Wait," Dex said, not quite believing his own ears, even though by now, he'd trust Aidan with his life (and his heart), "are you saying there's diamonds all over the North Pole?"

"All over the frozen tundra," Aidan said with a shrug. "How do you think we can pay for all those gifts? Some of them are magic, sure, but the diamonds we harvest? Those are a real moneymaker."

"You mine for these?"

"Oh, we don't *mine* for them," Aidan corrected with an adorably crooked grin, "we pick them up off the snow."

Dexter rolled his eyes at how ridiculous this was. "You North Pole elves are a wild bunch."

"That's what everyone's always telling us, but in reality, it's pretty boring up there," Aidan admitted. "I just don't know how this could've gotten in there. It's almost like . . ."

Aidan trailed off, like he didn't like the conclusion he'd come to. Like he didn't want to say it out loud.

But Dex, who didn't like what he didn't know, prompted, "Like what?"

"Like it was *put* there," Aidan said.

"Well, however it got there, we got it out," Dex said. Not particularly liking the conclusion that Aidan had drawn. "And now we gotta figure out if we were right and that was the problem."

"You think so?" Aidan sounded hopeful.

Dex was too, but then a similar wave of feeling that he'd had the moment Santa had arrived at the store crested over him.

Aidan was going to be leaving. Soon, if they had figured out the root of the problem.

And that realization, no matter which angle he viewed it from, hurt.

It hurt even more than it had an hour earlier, because now he'd spent that last hour with Aidan, and he liked him even more than he had before.

If that was even possible.

"I guess we'll find out," Dexter said, dropping the diamond into Aidan's hand, and taking the wrench, hooking up the hose again.

This time there was nothing to disrupt the flow of magic, and Dex watched with fascination as the energy spilled from the source into the engine, filling it with an unearthly glow.

"Looks good," Aidan said, peering in next to him. Despite his words, his voice sounded vaguely melancholy.

He was probably thinking of the same thing Dex was: with the sleigh fixed, there'd be no reason for him to stick around.

They were back to the same three hundred and sixty-five problem.

"Yeah, I think it'll start up," Dexter said. "Can you try it?"

"I think I remember how," Aidan said, and he climbed into the sleigh. Dex shouldn't have immediately felt his loss next to him, but he did.

This was going to be a real bitch.

Dex watched as Aidan hit a number of switches in a complicated pattern, and then on cue the engine roared to life, now that there was nothing to hold back the flow of magic.

"Well, this sucks," Aidan said, turning the engine off. He climbed down, and leaned against the hood, watching Dexter with a pained expression.

Dex knew how he felt. Because he was feeling the exact same goddamned thing.

"I wonder if I could convince Sam . . ."

But Aidan didn't get the rest of the sentence out before suddenly Sam was there, walking towards them from the mouth of the alley.

"Convince Sam to do?" Sam asked jovially. He glanced over at the engine, and his smile widened. "You've fixed it."

"Yeah," Aidan said. "There was a diamond in the line from the magic source to the engine, and weirdly, it wasn't like an unharvested diamond, all rough, like the sleigh might have picked it up on a test run, but smooth and polished. Like it belongs to someone."

"Let me see," Sam said, and held out his hand.

Aidan gave it to him, and Sam glanced at it for a second, before, to Dex's surprise, dropping it in his pocket.

"Glad you found that," Sam said, his words frustratingly vague. "I've been looking for it."

"Wait," Aidan said, the look in his eyes shocked, "that was *yours?*"

"Big thanks for finding it so quickly," Sam said, his own eyes twinkling with mischief. "You two make a great team."

"I guess we do," Dex said, though it somehow hurt even more to have someone else point it out, because of course, he'd known it would be true.

Just like he'd known, impossibly, from the first time he'd seen Aidan, that he would be important to him. That Dex's sun would rise and set around the unearthly glow in Aidan's beautiful green eyes.

Sam turned to Dexter. "You saved our mission," he said, "so I don't think it's too out of line to offer you a boon. Would you like to accompany us on our trip? And perhaps take a tour of the North Pole after? We'll say . . . a twenty-four-hour boon. That feels fair, don't you think?"

Dexter gaped. He didn't think at all. He just nodded, enthusiastically.

It wasn't everything he wanted, but it was . . . something.

Maybe it would hurt even more to say goodbye to Aidan at the end, but he'd get to see the North Pole. He was not only insatiably curious because of the elvish magic, but because this was where Aidan lived.

Maybe they'd even get a few minutes alone.

"You'd let him do that?" Aidan asked, awe in his voice. Like he'd wanted to ask for it, but hadn't known how to phrase the request.

"You two have been very helpful," Sam said seriously. "It's a fair boon, I believe."

"I'm honored to accept it," Dex said.

"Well, then," Sam said, "let's get ready to take off. We don't have much time to lose, as we have already had such a long delay."

"Wait," Aidan said, as he watched Dex start to put the engine cover back on, "I have a question."

Sam raised an eyebrow.

"The magic," Aidan said, "it didn't hurt Dex. In fact, it glowed even brighter."

"I didn't hear a question there," Sam said frustratingly.

Because if Dex was going to be honest, he was interested too.

Why *hadn't* the magic hurt him? Aidan had said he hadn't been sure what it would do, but it had done nothing *to* him, and instead he was the thing that had seemingly made it even more powerful.

"Edmund's always telling us that there isn't any record of what magic will do to humans, which is why we have to keep our distance," Aidan said slowly. "Is he wrong?"

Santa's eyes twinkled again. "You'd like that, wouldn't you?"

Aidan shot Sam a look. "Yes, but what I really want is the truth."

"The truth?" Sam hesitated. "It's complicated, but to simplify it, the magic is distilled belief, and since elves know the truth about the holiday and about me and my family, the magic is the most powerful when humans believe in me, and in the North Pole, and in Christmas."

"So when Dex believed and it felt that, it grew stronger," Aidan theorized.

As Dexter tightened the engine cover, he thought, *he never gives himself enough credit. He's smart as hell. I love that about him.*

Because he did.

Aidan was the whole package, and Dex wanted nothing more than him, beautifully wrapped, under his tree.

"That is a possibility," Sam said, but his smile made it clear that Aidan had hit the nail on the head.

"Then why does Edmund keep trying to keep elves and humans apart?" Aidan complained.

Dex knew he was also thinking of the three hundred and sixty-five problem. Still. Always.

"It's a powerful and uncertain merging, sometimes, but when it works together, it can be a beautiful thing," Sam said. "Like you and Dexter. Your feelings for each other are as bright as a star in the sky."

Dex swallowed hard. He'd known he wasn't alone in the way he felt, but it was a little gratifying to see Aidan flush red.

"And," Sam continued, "the right combination can bring incredible power to the community. My great-grandmother was human. Her husband, my ancestor, met her when he was delivering gifts, and look at how strong the magic in their blood has made me."

"So, sometimes it works, and sometimes it doesn't?" Aidan wondered.

"It's so powerful, sometimes the power can implode on itself," Sam said, "which is why Edmund is cautious. Perhaps he's overcautious. But when it works? There's nothing else like it."

When Aidan glanced over at him, Dex could feel the power in his gaze, and knew that Sam was right.

"Sometimes it's just right," Aidan suggested.

"Exactly," Sam said. "Are we all ready to go, Dexter?"

Dexter closed the lid to the engine compartment, and felt it snap shut. "Let's give it a whirl," he said.

"Excellent," Sam said. "Aidan—grab the tools. We need to get going."

Dex was just about to climb into the sleigh, when he realized just how small that bench seat was. Would all three of them fit?

Sam shot him a look, and did something with his fingers, and suddenly the sleigh was bigger, with a second seat behind the first.

"There," Sam said, gesturing to the back. "Now you two don't have to share with this old, boring man."

"You're Santa," Dexter said, trying not to gape in surprise at how easily Sam had just modified the sleigh. With merely a snap of his fingers.

"Still an old, boring man," Sam claimed. "Aidan, the *tools*."

Aidan shot Sam an amused look, and then made a complicated motion with his hands over the tool kit and it shrank back to its normal size. Dex wiped his hands on his jeans, picked up his coat, and followed Aidan into the sleigh.

Nothing, he knew, would ever be the same again.

Chapter Seven

Dexter had known, of course, that Aidan was an elf, and that every Christmas Eve he joined Santa on the sleigh, to deliver presents to the children of the world.

But it was one thing to be aware of such an extraordinary situation, and it was another entirely to experience it.

Sam handled the sleigh like he'd been born to do it, diving and dodging around buildings, only landing the sleigh briefly on rooftops to deliver gifts, the brightly decorated packages appearing from thin air, zipping from his fingers into any opening in the houses and condos and apartment buildings.

"Is it always like this?" Dexter asked as they stopped on one particularly breathtaking rooftop with an incredible view of the London skyline.

"The first year I was pretty much cold the whole damn time, but yeah," Aidan said, snuggling closer to Dex.

"I think I might have said I could keep you warm," Dex teased. "Am I doing a proper job of it?"

"A little too proper," Aidan said, turning towards him. "You're all the way over there."

All the way over there was maybe a few inches.

Dexter laughed.

"Didn't want Sam to feel too much like a third wheel," he said, as the man in question took off from the roof again in a dizzying rush.

Dexter didn't think he'd ever get used to that feeling of utter weightlessness, of the swoop in his stomach when the sleigh dipped and turned suddenly, Sam long since having discovered the best methods to navigate the big cities.

Of course, the cities, with their lights and skyscrapers, were incredible, but Dexter had equally enjoyed the open plains of South Dakota and Montana, the sparse beauty of the darkened plains, and the incredible light of the stars above them.

Not once had he been tempted to check his phone, which seemed like it was for the best as Aidan had warned him it wouldn't work.

"That's why we don't have them," Aidan had said when they'd first left Chicago, "the sleigh has a magical time-slowing mechanism, which allows Sam to traverse the world in a single evening. The magic messes with that kind of technology."

"But not others," Dex said, feeling curious even though he definitely wasn't an expert on the intersection of magic and technology.

But what he wouldn't give to take a closer look . . . to map the differences and the possibilities.

He'd said a dozen times already that he wanted a job where he could use his imagination.

Sam hasn't offered you a job, he reminded himself, and this one magical night might be the only time you ever get with Aidan. Don't ruin it by worrying about what you're going to do after graduation.

Aidan snuggled up closer as Sam flew the sleigh around Montmartre and then headed out past the buildings of Paris towards the French countryside.

"I never thought that this would be romantic," Aidan offered quietly, tipping his face up to Dex's.

"You just thought it was cold," Dex said.

"Well, it's *not* not cold, but it turns out that when you're with me, that's not what I'm thinking about. Not anymore."

"It's not what I'm thinking about either," Dex admitted. Everywhere he was pressed to Aidan felt tingly and alive, and surprisingly warm. He wanted to be stretched out with him, naked skin to naked skin, so he could feel that way everywhere.

But he'd already told himself that he wasn't going to go there —mentally or otherwise—with Sam in the sleigh.

It just felt too weird.

But he still wanted it.

Bad.

He had high hopes that when they finally got back to the North Pole, he could convince Aidan to show him where he lived—though the chances of Aidan not physically dragging him back to his room seemed small, considering the heat in the elf's eyes whenever their gazes met.

And then there'd been the passion in his kisses.

They definitely wanted each other.

Dex told himself that good things came to those who waited, and that eventually, he'd get to unwrap Aidan like a present he'd been dying to open.

Every once in awhile, Aidan had to nimbly climb onto the front seat to fix a problem or consult about a problem with a present delivery, but to Dex's eyes, considering how many gifts they were delivering, the issues were few and far between. Not only that, but Aidan fixed them efficiently and easily, usually with only a suggestion or a recalibration of one of the magical devices.

"You're good at this," Dex told him as he returned to their seat, the sleigh flying over Singapore.

"What? No," Aidan said with a self-deprecating laugh. "I'm still learning. Maybe someday I'll be actually good. At least that's what Edmund keeps telling me."

"You're good at this *now*," Dex insisted, wrapping an arm around him and, despite Sam's presence in the front seat, dragging him those last few inches until they were pressed together, snuggling under the fur-lined blanket. "I know I've said it before, but you don't give yourself enough credit. You showed up in the North Pole less than two years ago, and you're practically running it."

Aidan's eyes gleamed. "Don't let Edmund hear you say that."

"I'd tell him to back off, to give you a bit of breathing space," Dex said slowly, "but you're already doing that."

"Yeah, I do, sometimes. I think I've given him a few extra gray hairs, for sure."

"But it's probably good for him," Dex persisted. "It seems like he needed a bit of shaking up. Complacency doesn't do anyone any favors."

"You've been paying attention, haven't you?" Aidan bit his lower lip, and Dexter gave himself a lot of credit for not dragging him even closer, for covering his mouth with his own.

It was not easy to be this close to someone he was so crazy about, who he wanted so desperately, and *wait*.

But he was doing it.

If he missed his one and only sleigh ride because he was too busy fantasizing about what he wanted to do to Aidan, well . . . he might regret it. Eventually.

"What gave it away?" Dex said, trying to drag his mind back to the conversation and away from what Aidan might look like —*feel* like—under his clothes.

"Maybe all those emails we exchanged," Aidan teased.

"Maybe you're not good at the engineering component," Dex admitted, because the last thing he wanted Aidan to believe was that Dex just wanted him physically. He wanted all of him. He *liked* all of him. His smarts and the unique way his brain worked. His dry sense of humor. The magic that sparked from his fingertips. Every part of Aidan that made up the whole was worth admiring and worshipping. "But you said it yourself, you're good at logistics, from back when you were at Tír na nÓg, and now you're working on the biggest logistical problem in the world."

Aidan tilted his head, considering this. "I hadn't thought of it that way before," he said softly. "I just . . . I didn't get it. I'm not sure I'll ever care about Christmas the way the other North Pole elves do, but it's growing on me. And when I thought Sam might not be able to deliver the presents . . . I realized just how much it meant."

"I know I said I'd tell you this later, but I guess there's no good time like the present. The shirt?" Dex said, gesturing to where the Bah Humbug was hidden by his jacket and then the blanket. "I wasn't trying to be ironic. Before I met you, I hated Christmas."

Aidan looked concerned. "Why?"

"My parents got divorced when I was ten. They'd never spent much time with me, but when the divorce happened, I thought, that'll change. It didn't." Dex heard how wry his voice was. Some things you had to laugh about—or you might cry about them instead. And the fractious relationship he'd always had with his parents . . . that definitely fell into that particular category. "Instead of spending time with me, they tried to outdo each other with gifts. The fancier the toy, the more expensive the gadget, the better. Christmas was . . . well, it was the worst.

I figured out that the presents didn't mean anything. They didn't mean they cared about me, they were just another way to compete with each other."

"And all you wanted was them to see you, to love you," Aidan said softly. He dropped his head onto Dex's shoulder. "I'm so sorry that happened to you."

"Before you showed up, I thought Christmas was a fake, materialistic holiday, full of crap about people pretending to care about each other, but only really caring about themselves."

"What changed your mind?"

Dex laughed. "You, well, you *and* Santa."

"Because it's not fake, after all?"

"Yeah, that's part of it, obviously, but then I thought, after you left and we started to email, how is it really any different? You're still giving gifts."

"But it's more than that," Aidan said and Dex nodded, glad he understood. "Sometimes it *is* about showing someone that you care. That you see them. That you remember them. That's what we're doing." Aidan added. "What we're *trying* to do, anyway."

"It's a pretty good goal," Dex agreed. "Anyway, I still wish holidays focused less on the materialistic and more on people—but what you're doing? It's a start."

"Dexter, you make an excellent point," Sam said, and Dex jumped a little. Surprised, though he supposed he shouldn't have been, that Sam had been listening to their conversation.

Good thing he hadn't whispered all the things he wanted to do to Aidan later into his ear.

"Thanks?" Dex said.

He supposed he should be embarrassed that he'd just been caught wishing the holidays were less materialistic by Santa himself—but Sam didn't seem particularly offended. Just thoughtful.

"It's something we're always working on," Sam admitted. "And ways to keep belief high, so we can continue to bring magic to the world."

"Is that a problem?"

"In this era of cell phones and the internet and the TikTok?" Sam asked wryly. "Harder than you'd imagine. We do okay but we could always do better. I keep a sharp eye out for new ideas, so if you have any . . ."

"I'll be sure to pass them on to Aidan here," Dexter said.

"I'm sure he'll make sure they get to me," Sam said, with an extra twinkle in his blue eyes. "If only because I think he enjoys giving Edmund a hard time."

"I'd guess that it's pretty mutual with them," Dexter theorized, and Sam laughed.

"Yes, you do know him," Sam observed when he'd finally stopped chuckling. "Not that there was any doubt in my mind."

"About that," Aidan said, leaning forward and joining in the conversation. "How *did* you know about me and Dex?"

"Aidan," Sam said seriously, "I'm Santa. I know when you're sleeping, and when you're awake, and definitely whether you've been bad or good."

"I see your point," Aidan grumbled.

But Dexter couldn't stop smiling, even when they wrapped up the night, flying over the vast expanse of the ocean, making the last of their deliveries to the little tiny islands scattered across it.

It was warm enough, even, that Aidan felt comfortable shedding the fur-lined cloak, and from the way his eyes brightened in interest in the beaches as they flew over, Dex couldn't help but wish that someday he'd get to take him here, for a tropical vacation.

Was that even allowed? He doubted it. But there had to be some benefit, besides this twenty-four-hour boon, in saving Christmas, right?

"So," Dex said as they flew further and further north, the blanket creeping up their bodies as it grew colder, "do you finally feel like you've earned your title now?"

Aidan looked at him with adorable confusion. "What?"

"You saved Christmas. I know you've never felt like the Savior type. That you even *could* and you did, tonight."

"No, I didn't. I . . . I pulled a rock out of a hose," Aidan said. "A rock in a hose *you* found. I'm not the Christmas Savior. That's just a . . . silly prophecy that doesn't mean anything."

For someone so smart, it was amazing how dense Aidan could be sometimes.

Dex was far gone enough that he found even that pretty dang cute.

"I think it means more than you realize," Dex said slowly. "And even if it was me who found the rock, who do you think found me? Who thought to ask me to help? If you hadn't, you might still be sitting in that alley in Chicago, instead of heading back to the North Pole."

Aidan tilted his head. "You really want to believe that I'm the Savior because I . . . know you? It seems they should have called you the Savior, then." He didn't sound bitter or regretful at all about this particular suggestion; in fact, it sounded like he'd have preferred it that way.

And Dex got it. A little, anyway.

It would be hard to have your whole life decided for you, based on things you had no control over

Aidan had had his whole life turned inside out and nobody had ever asked him if he'd wanted the title.

"I'm not an elf though," Dex teased. "I don't have these cute-as-hell ears." He touched them now, and he made a mental note of the way Aidan's eyes rolled back into his head. He was definitely going to need to re-visit that idea later.

Hopefully not too much later.

"You ready to head back to the North Pole?" Sam asked from the front of the sleigh.

"Never been readier," Aidan said with a slow grin, the look in his eyes making Dex's fingers twitch with how much he wanted to touch him.

There was nothing he enjoyed more than taking something amazing, taking it apart, figuring out just how it ticked, and then putting it together even better than before.

With Aidan? It was going to be incredible and epic and probably life-altering.

Would Dex ever again be able to settle for mediocre sex?

Probably not.

Dex knew he wouldn't even want to.

He was going to want Aidan, each and every time, and they hadn't even done more than kiss yet.

"Yeah, I can't wait to see it," Dex said. "Aidan's told me a lot about it." He hesitated. "Though really, you've told me about more what it *isn't* like than what it is."

"Maybe I was just hoping you'd come here someday and I'd get to surprise you," Aidan said in a light teasing voice.

"I think," Dex said, dropping his head down almost by Aidan's ear. Feeling him shiver under the near-touch. "I think you're going to surprise me in all the best kind of ways."

"In *every* kind of way," Aidan promised, and then, emerging out of the sky, taking Dex's breath away was the thing that had actually done more than anything else to keep them apart.

The magical barrier, glowing faintly blue and white, preventing satellites and researchers and tourists from every figuring out what kind of extraordinary community lay underneath.

Santa flew the sleigh right through it, the speed filling Dex with exhilaration as the wind whipped through his hair. It was cold, just like Aidan had said, but the temperature, just like the elf next to him, made him feel more alive than he ever had before.

The moment they passed through the barrier, Dex felt the thrill of it right along his spine, almost like electricity working its way through his body.

"My great-grandmother, she used to travel back and forth, just to feel it," Sam said with a twinkling smile at Dex as he pulled the sleigh up and then around, finally landing it on the diamond-encrusted pad. "You'll know it's here, if you ever come back, but you won't be able to get in. Our magic is the key to the lock, so to speak."

"Welcome to the North Pole," Aidan said, pulling him into a tight hug. "I can't wait to show you everything."

There was already a crowd gathered there, lots of elves staring at him like maybe he'd grown that second head after all.

And that it was dyed bright neon green.

"I don't think," Aidan said under his breath as they climbed out of the sleigh, "that most of them have ever seen a human before."

It was clear from the way they were all staring at him, eyes huge and wide, mouths dropped open, dressed in a variation of Aidan's tunic and leggings, in a variety of reds, golds, greens, and silvers, that they *hadn't*.

"This should be fun, then," Dexter said. He suddenly had an inkling of an idea of why Aidan had walked into his store last year and had frozen solid for a good minute. It was weird, to be in a place that was both familiar and very, very different.

"Fellow North Pole elves," Sam said, suddenly his kind, soft voice morphing into one that positively *boomed*, like he was a human version of a loudspeaker. *Magic*, Dex thought, *you're never gonna get used to that.* "It's my greatest honor to introduce you to the man who helped our Christmas Savior fix the sleigh tonight, making it possible for me to deliver toys to the children of the world."

A cheer went up in the crowd, and though Dex could see that some of them looked confused or intrigued, nobody looked upset. They all looked . . . happy. Surprisingly happy. *Welcome to the North Pole.*

Then suddenly there was one who wasn't.

He was a little shorter than Aidan, who had claimed on more than one occasion that he was *tall* for an elf, and he was dressed in a practical brown tunic, his only concession to the holiday a massive corsage of holly and poinsettias pinned to his shoulder, and he was frowning.

Specifically, he was frowning at Aidan, and at Dex too, because the force of his glare encompassed both of them.

This had to be Edmund.

Dex had always told himself that if he met the elf-in-charge who'd made Aidan's life a lot tougher than it needed to be, that he'd pay him back.

Now that he was in front of Edmund, he revised his plan.

"Hi there," he said, pasting on his friendliest smile and walking right over to Edmund. He stuck out his hand and grinned brighter.

Edmund *glowered*.

It was a whole-litter-of-kittens kind of awesome.

Dex felt rather than saw Aidan walk up next to him.

"Aidan," Edmund said stiffly, completely ignoring Dex's outstretched hand. "What is this about the sleigh being broken and what is . . . *he*?"

Aidan smiled broadly. "It broke down in Chicago, but we fixed it with Dexter's help. That's Dexter, by the way. He's my friend."

"Friend?" Edmund looked like he was tasting out a particularly unpleasant word.

For a second Dex was afraid it was because he didn't like that he and Aidan were romantically involved because they were both men, but then he realized, that wasn't it at all. It was because he was a *human*.

"Yes," Aidan said. Glanced over at Dex, warmth in his eyes. "And so much more." He reached out and took Dex's hand and squeezed it tightly.

"I can't believe you told him our secrets. Showed him the way to the North Pole," Edmund said.

"That was all Sam, you can yell at him," Aidan said flippantly. "I know the gala is in a few hours, but until then, I'm going to be showing Dexter around the North Pole."

"Yell at Sam! Around the North Pole!" came out Edmund's strangled response.

He was still spluttering when they turned around, and then after walking a distance, turned a corner, around the edge of the sleigh barn, and Dex felt the breath go out of his lungs.

Much the way it had when he'd seen Aidan for the very first time.

"It's . . ." Dex considered himself a fairly intelligent person, who was also pretty decent at expressing himself, but the sight before him left him breathless and *wordless*.

The North Pole was laid out like a priceless jewel, quaint and brightly painted buildings rising out of the sparkling, icy ground. Strands of Christmas lights twinkled everywhere, in what would normally be the dark gloom of coming dawn, but the sky was illuminated instead by the soft bluish-white glow of the magical barrier.

"How is it that I can see that and nobody else can?" Dex asked.

Trust a question about how something worked to unstick his tongue.

"Because you already know and believe in magic," Aidan said matter-of-factly. "If you were like every other human, who rejects the possibility, you could walk right up to it and never know it was there."

"So people who don't believe or don't know are blind to it? What if they just . . . happen to wander through it?"

They were growing closer to the village now. Not only were the strands of lights crisscrossing above them, there was a brightly decorated tree shining with ornaments and lights on the front stoop of every cottage. Then there was the holly and mistletoe hanging over every doorway, swags and ribbon decorating practically every other surface.

It was a spectacular—if a bit *busy*—sight. Dex understood a little how Aidan, coming from Tír na nÓg, might feel initially overwhelmed by *so much* Christmas spirit.

"Do you really think humans are up here, just . . . wandering around?" Aidan teased.

"No, but I still want to know." His insatiable curiosity was incredibly piqued by this place.

And the elf walking next to him.

"I believe, if I remember my lessons—this was during the beginning, right when we first started emailing, and I won't lie,

I walked around in kind of a love-drunk haze—correctly, then the magic transports them to the other side, with them none the wiser."

"Fascinating." Dex grinned. "Love-drunk haze, huh?"

Aidan flushed. "Forget I said that."

"I don't think I want to," Dex said, squeezing his fingers. "In fact, I wanna hear *more* about it."

"If I get going," Aidan promised, "you're not going to get the full North Pole experience."

"Hmm, that's a tough decision. Romancing you—or letting you romance *me*—or getting to tour the magical North Pole on Christmas? That is a tough call." Dexter shot Aidan a look. Promising him everything. "Can I have both? Pretty please, wrapped in your prettiest paper?"

Aidan slowed and then stopped, pulling Dex to face him. He reached up and pressed a kiss to his cheek. "What kind of North Pole elf would I be if I denied you anything you wanted on Christmas?"

Chapter Eight

It was extraordinary, seeing the North Pole through Dexter's eyes.

He wanted to know how every single thing worked, all the magic, all the mechanisms, each piece of technology, *everything*.

His insatiable curiosity made Aidan curious, all over again, and he couldn't help but remember how he'd felt that first week he'd been at the North Pole, when he'd felt the charm of the village and its participants as a visceral thing, and he'd actually *wanted* to figure out how it all worked. Then it had gone sour, with the hero worship for something he didn't think he deserved, and Edmund's incessant, boring lectures, turning even the most magical of experiences into something humdrum.

But Dexter brought it all back.

"What do you want to do first?" he asked, as they finished touring the main village proper. He'd shown Dex the enormous Christmas tree in the center of the square, and the surrounding cottages, as well as the different workshops where toys and many other things were created. Dex hadn't believed that they'd managed to erect an even *bigger* tree in the gathering hall, ready for the Christmas Gala tonight, but he would see it in a few hours with his own two eyes.

"First?" Dex's eyes were huge, amazed, *enchanted*.

Aidan had never thought he'd be lucky enough to give this to him—he'd hoped, and he'd dreamed, but he hadn't been sure—and it was already even more incredible than he'd ever fantasized it could be.

Love, already taking root, bloomed in his heart.

"Well, I was thinking we'd stop by Billy's bakery, see if we could scrounge some meat pies, maybe even some of his famous eclairs. He might even let us decorate some cookies for you to take back, for Mr. Husseini and for Jonathan, and then I thought, you have to visit the toy shop, and of course, where George makes his magic snow globes, and . . . what else?"

"I . . ." Dex took a deep breath. "I want to know how Santa *knows*."

"When you're sleeping and when you're awake?" Aidan teased.

"No," Dex said. "How he knows what each child wants. What do you do with the letters?"

"Ahhh, of course you do." Aidan was kicking himself a little for not thinking of the post office, and the Wish Book, because of course Dexter would want to know how *that* worked.

"And after," Dex added with a lopsided grin, "all those other things, too. Definitely the eclairs. And the snow globes! Can I take one of those home too?"

"Not . . . not *technically*," Aidan hedged, but he already knew he'd figure out a way. George was nice. Amenable, even. He could probably be bribed.

"And then," Dex said, suddenly right in Aidan's space, big and warm and smelling like a pine forest. He cupped Aidan's cheek with his hand, equally big and equally warm, and then they were kissing, like they would never stop. Aidan's brain spluttered and then just plain stopped. Then Dex's tongue brushed his, Aidan's blood fizzing, and he wanted to say *screw everything else, do you want to screw me?*

But then Dex was pulling away. "And then," he repeated, his voice low and gravelly, making Aidan ache with arousal, "you're going to show me your room, okay?"

"Okay," Aidan said, nodding like a puppet on a string.

Thought was . . . well, thought was overrated.

"The letters first, then?" Dex asked hopefully, and Aidan remembered that, *oh yes, they were supposed to be doing something that wasn't kissing.*

"Letters first," Aidan agreed, tugging on Dex's hand, leading him in the direction of the post office and the Wish Book.

This was special, and Dex was really going to love this.

"So," Dex said, a crease appearing between his dark brows, like he was thinking *very* hard about how all this worked, "what you're saying is that the letters are entered here, by hand, into this book, and then Santa . . . *absorbs* it?"

Michael, the head of the post office, free because he'd already done the lion's share of his work for the year, nodded enthusiastically. "You have it, sir, that's exactly right."

"Could I write something in the book?"

"Have you wished for something this year? A wish you sent to Santa?" Michael asked archly. "As you're only allowed one wish per year. Magic's rules."

"Magic has rules?" Dexter asked, amused. "And no, no, not to Santa, at least."

"Well, then," Michael said, pulling a pen from his pocket, "you are free, of course, to write your own wish in. The elves here do, sometimes."

"Have you?" Dexter asked, turning to Aidan, curiosity lighting his eyes.

"Not yet," Aidan admitted. Edmund had kept him very busy this year, and last year, he'd been too overwhelmed to even *think* about making a wish for Santa to fulfill.

"Do you want to?" Michael asked, brandishing a second pen.

Aidan was tempted to ask him just how many pens he had secreted about his person, but then he was in charge of the post office. He probably magicked them out of thin air.

"I'm good, thanks, got all the magic I need right here," Aidan said, glancing up at Dex, who smiled broadly.

Aidan probably could have made the time to come over here and enter his own wish into the book, but he'd been afraid of wishing for what he really, *truly*, wanted, because he wasn't sure even Santa would have found it possible.

But now it was, because Dex was standing right next to him.

"Well, I'll wish for both of us, then," Dex said, taking the pen from George.

"It's not polite to watch," Michael reminded him, as he turned away.

Aidan really wanted to see what Dex wrote, but Michael was right. It was really impolite to stare, and unfortunately, when Dex finished writing his wish with a final flourish on the old, wrinkled pages, the book absorbed the ink with a quick flash of light, the letters glowing bright gold, and then they were gone.

The only place they existed was in Santa's memory.

"I want to know how Santa keeps it all straight," Dex said, returning the pen to Michael.

"Magic," Michael said knowingly. "It makes so many things possible."

"It does seem to," Dex agreed. "Thank you so much for your time."

"It's my pleasure, young man," Michael said kindly. "And thank you, Aidan, dear, for bringing him by. It was a delight to meet a human."

"Really?" Dex questioned. "Some of the elves don't seem to know quite what to make of me."

"Some humans, yes, but you? Never. You're a good man. Curious but not destructive. And respectful. And Aidan here, well, he clearly cares about you a lot." Michael's eyes twinkled, not unlike how Santa's had, when it had become clear he'd known all along about their email exchange.

"It was an honor to meet you as well, and thank you for letting me write my wish," Dex said. He turned to Aidan. "Are we off to Billy's now?"

"Oh," Michael cried, "have a meat pie for me. They are *splendid*."

When they walked back out into the snowy path, letting the door to the post office shut behind them, Dex turned to Aidan with a bright smile. "That was freaking amazing," he said, "the way everything works? It's just brilliant."

"That's magic for you," Aidan said.

"I get though," Dexter said, as Aidan led him towards Billy's bakery, "why you didn't feel so comfortable here at first. Everyone's so . . . well, so into Christmas and magic and it's not like you weren't, but you were into a different kind of magic."

"It was different," Aidan agreed quietly.

"And the way people stare at you," Dex added, his voice soft. "They stare at me, too, but they're staring differently at you. Like . . . like they want to worship you, but not like I'm planning on worshipping you."

"Yeah, it gets old," Aidan admitted, trying not to flush at Dex's other observation.

"I bet it does."

"It feels different though, with you here," Aidan pointed out. Thinking, not for the first time, what it might feel like if he *always* had Dexter here. Dex seemed to really enjoy being here, he was having a great time, and the other elves were pretty welcoming. This might . . . Aidan didn't want to get his hopes up . . . but he already knew that before Dex's twenty-four hours were up, he was going to ask him if he could stay.

He didn't know what Dex would say but he was hoping—except it was so much more than just hope at this point. It was something bigger and brighter, something so much more fervent than simply a wish, which was why he hadn't written it down in the Wish Book.

"Really?" Dex sounded surprised.

Aidan paused at the doorstep to Billy's bakery. "It isn't exactly a secret that I haven't been happy here."

"Yeah, but you seemed to be fitting in better. You made friends. At least there were elves who didn't treat you so differently." Dex's words were kind but they still stung. "I'd call them friends, anyway."

Had he been adjusting, and hadn't even realized it?

Aidan guessed he didn't resent the North Pole the way he had when he'd first arrived. He'd even learned to enjoy some of the facets of their Christmas celebrations. There were way too many of them, but they could be enjoyable.

And this year he'd felt like he'd finally *found* the much-vaunted spirit of Christmas—but so much of that anticipatory excitement had been wrapped up in getting to see Dexter again.

What if Dex was right, and even without him, he was really getting used to being a North Pole elf?

Aidan didn't know how he felt about that.

"I guess . . ." he said slowly. "I guess you might be right."

"I know I'm right," Dex said, an adorably smug smile creeping onto his face. "As long as you know it, too."

Aidan smacked him on the arm. "Let's go get some food and steal some cookies from Billy."

Dexter pushed the door open—Aidan had led them to the back and not the front door, on purpose, because there was no way, this close to the gala, that Billy would still be open to regular visitors—and as they walked in, Billy looked up from one of his long wooden work counters with a smear of flour on his cheek, and a disgruntled expression on his face.

"What are you doing here?" he demanded to know.

"Just wanted to stop in, and . . ." That was all Aidan got out before Billy's eyes grew wide and then impossibly wider.

"Is this . . . You're not an elf, you're a human."

Dexter nodded, a little sheepishly.

Billy shot Aidan a hard look. "You weren't asking about another elf, from Tír na nÓg, were you?"

"No," Aidan admitted. "No, I wasn't."

"Ha! I knew it." Billy dusted his hands off and approached them. "I'm Billy," he said, and he and Dex shook hands briefly.

"Dex," the other man said, introducing himself. "I hear you're the best baker in the North Pole."

"Best or most gullible," Billy teased, shooting Aidan another look. "Either one works. You two here for something to eat before the gala, because I'm telling you . . ."

"Just a few meat pies and maaaaaybe a few cookies?" Aidan wheedled.

"You're in luck that my gingerbread display is already done and down at the hall," Billy said. "Here, I'll get you set up over here, in this corner." He showed them an empty workstation, and then was off, grabbing various items from the gigantic warming ovens that lined one wall.

"Here," he said, depositing a plate full of pies on the table, and then another of cookies, crisp and sugary around the edges. "You eat, and I'll grab you some frosting. Because you'll want to decorate those."

"We will?" Dex seemed surprised at Billy's insistence.

"Oh, you *will*," Billy said firmly. "It's not a Christmas cookie if it's not decorated."

"What about . . ." But Aidan was already putting a finger across Dex's mouth, sure that he was going to say *something* that would send Billy—who had strong feelings about desserts—into some kind of lecture.

He liked Billy. He did. But his eyes usually glazed over by the fiftieth minute of snowballs versus slice and bake.

"I'll be right back," Billy said with a quick confident nod.

Aidan removed his fingers and Dex shot him an amused look which heated him all the way through.

"You should . . . uh . . . try the pies," Aidan said awkwardly.

Dex smiled, and grabbed one, inhaling its rich scent as he took a bite.

"Oh my God," he exclaimed as he chewed. "That's amazing."

"Billy's a genius. A bit of an eccentric genius, but a genius nonetheless," Aidan said, taking another meat pie from the plate.

"These are just . . . really fucking good," Dex said, still chewing another mouthful. "He makes these here?"

"With practically no help," Aidan said. "He doesn't like a lot of elves underfoot, he says."

"And," Dexter said, bringing up the thing that Aidan kinda wished he had forgotten, "you told him about me. And he thought I was an elf? From Tír na nÓg?"

"I couldn't very well tell him you were a human I met in Chicago at a convenience store, could I?"

Dexter grinned. "I'm not interested in what you couldn't tell him, I'm interested in what you *did* tell him."

"He's dating another elf named Finn," Aidan said. "I just wanted some . . . well, some advice, if you must know."

"About?" Dexter had finished his first pie and was now working on his second, crumbs from the flaky dough falling to the countertop. A morsel of spiced beef joined them and Aidan felt zero compunction about grabbing it and popping it in his mouth.

"Does it matter?" Aidan said flippantly. He didn't want to tell Dex that he'd been trying to figure out a way for him to come here, and to *stay* here. It was still soon.

"Yeah, it matters." Dex's voice and expression had gone serious.

"It wasn't bad okay? It was a good thing, I'm just . . ." Aidan hesitated. "Not ready to talk about it just yet."

"Okay," Dex said. "But the moment you do . . ."

"You'll know," Aidan said, wrapping his arm around Dex's waist and giving him a quick hug.

"No canoodling in the bakery!" Billy barked out as he returned, holding a large container full of pastry bags filled with brightly colored frosting.

"Not sure I've ever heard that particular rule," Aidan teased him. "What about Finn? Surely you don't keep *him* at an arm's length when he's here."

Billy shot him an unimpressed look. "Finn doesn't usually come here. You know you're the only elf I tolerate here on a regular basis, because you're not . . ."

"Too much?" Aidan grinned. "I know."

"I think he's just right," Dexter declared, and Billy smiled.

"I knew I liked you," he said, setting the bin of frosting down on the table. "Now, feel free to decorate however you wish.

Have fun! Be creative!"

Aidan raised an eyebrow. "Be creative?"

Billy waved a hand. "Do your best. It doesn't matter what they look like, as long as you're happy with them. That's the spirit of it, right?"

"The spirit?" Dex asked under his breath after Billy had walked away, back to his regular workspace, where it looked like he was rolling out cinnamon rolls.

"It's like . . . a thing here," Aidan said, trying not to roll his eyes. "Like this whole Christmas spirit lives in you and you can use it to inspire others, and bring love and joy to others. That's what this whole community is built around. Spirit."

"Ah," Dex said. "And that's why you feel less than, sometimes, isn't it? Because you don't always feel it yourself."

"I'm the Elf Who Will Save Christmas," Aidan said, nodding, "I should be brimming with it, but I'm not. Not like the others."

"I think you need to give yourself a break. Your whole life changed less than two years ago. Expecting something that these elves have spent a whole lifetime developing is asking a lot out of yourself."

Aidan sighed and leaned his head against Dex's shoulder. "Why are you so smart?"

"It's a gift," Dex teased. "Now, show me how we're supposed to do this."

"Decorate the cookies?"

"Yeah, you've done this before, right? You mentioned spending time here with Billy in the bakery."

"I did," Aidan said, grabbing a pastry bag filled with bright red frosting, checking the knot to make sure the end was totally closed and wouldn't explode everywhere.

Easiest way to look like there'd been a particularly grisly murder at the bakery.

And Aidan only knew that because he'd been lucky enough to experience it once already.

Since that day and Billy's subsequent lecture, he always checked the frosting bags.

"Why did you do that?" Dexter asked, picking up his own bag, filled with emerald green.

"Check the knot? Gotta make sure it hasn't loosened over time," Aidan said putting his own bag down to double-check Dex's bag. "Otherwise, you're going to end up with frosting all over you when it squirts out the back."

"Shit," Dexter said, giggling a little under his breath. "Does that really happen?"

"It could and it did, once," Aidan said. "Which is why I always check the knots."

"Good to remember," Dex said, and Aidan wasn't surprised to see him check the knot again after Aidan handed him back his frosting. "Now, how do I do this?"

"You just . . ." Aidan demonstrated by swirling red icing all over the ornament-shaped cookie. "Like this. It's not so hard once you get the right motion."

"Yeah?" Dexter was grinning down at him, the smile so bright and sharp and knowing, it hit Aidan right in the stomach, arousal blooming through him.

"Hey, quit it," Aidan said, elbowing him softly in the ribs. But he didn't really mean it—and it was clear Dex didn't think so either.

"Yeah, you love it," Dex teased. "I'll be plenty happy to help you perfect your motion later."

"How much later?" Aidan asked plaintively, even though he was the one who'd designed their North Pole tour, wanting

Dex to see everything—and not just because he knew he'd enjoy it, but because Aidan knew he couldn't ask him to stay if he didn't know exactly what the North Pole had to offer. Where, exactly, Dexter could fit in, if he moved here.

Dexter laughed. "Soon, I hope? There's not too many more stops, right? And then the gala thing?"

Aidan leaned in, pushing himself up on his tiptoes so his mouth fit nearly over Dex's ear. "I think . . ." he murmured, "we should be very naughty, and skip the gala."

Dexter's eyes widened. "Really? Aren't you like some super special elf? Won't they miss you? Aren't you afraid you'll end up on Santa's Naughty List?"

"Maybe, but I don't care. I get twenty-four hours with you, and . . ." Aidan hesitated, taking a deep breath. "I don't want to waste a moment of it. Not a single second. Especially not making small talk with elves I don't care about. Not the way I care about you."

Dexter's expression grew soft. "I care about you, too," he said.

"Then it's decided," Aidan said feeling the beginning of something that felt like excitement, or might be nerves, blooming deep inside, "we'll go to George's for the snow globes, and then . . . back to my place?"

Dexter's smile was slow and sweet, and Aidan's heart began to beat a little bit faster. "I like the sound of that a lot. Sounds better than any gala. Our own private celebration."

As their eyes met, Aidan found that he couldn't agree more.

"That was actually more fun than I thought it'd be," Dex said as they left the bakery, mouth full of sugar cookie. They were the best cookies he'd ever tasted, though he supposed that bar wasn't particularly high because he normally ate Oreos and Chips Ahoy from a package.

Compared to those, this tasted like the most glorious intersection between sugar and butter and vanilla. He could *die* eating these cookies, and he'd still probably take another one.

Of course if he did perish, he'd never get to sample something else . . .

And that, Dex thought, glancing over at Aidan next to him, would be the *real* loss.

"What did you think it would be like?" Aidan wondered, as he shifted the bag of cookies Billy had packed up from them from one hand to the other, taking Dex's and squeezing it lightly.

"I'm not sure, but I've never really baked anything. I guess we didn't bake today, not truly, but the decorating? That was fun. I really enjoyed making Billy's head look like it was going to explode, when I decorated that one cookie in black and orange."

Aidan snickered. "That *was* hilarious. I thought he was going to snatch the frosting bag right out of your hand."

"But he didn't," Dex said proudly.

Aidan nudged him with his shoulder as they walked towards the shop where he'd said George created the magical snow globes. "That's because you told him you were all about the spirit of self-expression."

"Yes, I did." It had been almost more fun than laughing himself—getting Aidan to burst out into hysterical laughter.

He'd be lying to himself if he said he didn't want to do it all the time. He'd said, just a few hours ago, at the beginning of what had turned out to be the most incredible night of his life, that he wanted more with Aidan than a few minutes stolen every three hundred and sixty-five days. But the other thing that this night had made him realize was that they truly, irrevocably, lived in two different worlds.

Aidan's world had magic and whimsy and *Santa*.

Dex was supposed to be looking for a job, or committing to one of the handful that had fallen into his lap. He was supposed to be finding a new place to live with Jonathan. Doing the inventory for the new year in Mr. Husseini's shop. His life wasn't *bad*, but it also wasn't this fantastical confection of a dream.

And because Dex was always trying to figure out how things worked, and make them work better, he didn't know how to reconcile these two different worlds, no matter how he turned them this way and that.

You'll figure it out, because you have to figure it out, Dex told himself firmly, *and don't you dare let your confusion spoil what's been the best time of your life.*

"Here we are," Aidan said, guiding them into George's workshop.

Outside there'd been a hanging wood sign, decorated with a globe that literally *glowed*. He would've asked Aidan how it worked, because he *always* wanted to know, but then Aidan was pushing him inside and that question was supplanted with about a thousand others.

Because George's snow globes didn't just have a glowy sign, they *all* glowed.

"Wow," Dexter said, turning around slowly, trying to take in every inch of the work space. There were long wooden tables, much like Billy's bakery, but instead of being covered with flour and sugar and icing, these were strewn with tools, and every few feet there was a globe, emanating an incredible whitish-blue glow from within, like the glass itself was magical.

And inside, Dex saw, as he took a step closer, were scenes. Christmas scenes, some of the North Pole and some that must have taken the human world as inspiration. There were Christmas trees, mistletoe, holly wreaths and little red trucks, festooned with lights. And even though these were just dioramas, placed inside the globes, they felt *real*, like Dex could reach out and touch one. Could *go* there himself, with only a thought and a wish and a dream.

"It's pretty amazing, isn't it?" Aidan said. "George gave me a Tír na nÓg snow globe for the solstice celebration this year. It's got gold coins and lots of polished black cauldrons and a rainbow and even a tiny leprechaun."

"I remember you saying it was amazing," Dex said. Aidan's email describing the snow globe had been over-the-top, even for Aidan, and Dex had assumed that the rhapsodic nature had been due to Aidan missing Tír na nÓg, not the actual craftsmanship.

But now he was revising his opinion.

"When I shake it, and hold it in my hands, sometimes I can even feel like I'm back there, chasing rainbows." Aidan's voice was wistful.

"Aidan!" An elf, wizened with age, appeared in the doorway at the far end of the room. "Didn't know you'd be stopping back tonight."

"I wanted to introduce you to my friend, Dexter, and show him your incredible work," Aidan said.

George hobbled into the room, supporting much of his weight on a cane crafted from a twisted stick, the wood shiny and clearly well-used.

"Ah, so this is your friend that everyone has been talking about," George said knowingly.

Aidan rolled his eyes. "I don't know how gossip spreads so fast here."

"You and Santa show up from delivering gifts with a strapping young man," George said with a wheezing cackle, "you have to expect the news is going to spread like wildfire."

"I suppose. Well, Dex, this is George, our resident snow globe expert—really, he's a magician."

Dexter reached out and shook the elf's hand. "Magician? Is that what makes these so amazing, so lifelike? Magic?"

"Some of it, yes," George said, nodding. "But it is a well-practiced skill, too."

Dex's attention was caught by a particular globe, near George's right elbow. It contained a cityscape, glowing with lights, with a tiny sleigh and an even tinier Santa sitting in it. This one wasn't powered by a magical engine, but by the reindeer.

He felt like all he had to do was close his eyes and he would be back in that alley, and then in the sky, flying over the lights of Chicago, cuddled close with Aidan.

It was a memory of a lifetime, and it was like George had plucked it right from his brain, before it ever could have happened, and replicated the exact feel of it.

"That one, I thought you might like that," George said.

Aidan peered at it closer, but Dex hadn't managed to tear his eyes off it since he'd spotted it.

"I just . . . I can't comprehend how this is done, even with magic," Dex murmured under his breath.

"Dex is an engineer," Aidan explained to George. "He likes to know how things work."

"Ah, I thought I sensed a fellow tinkerer," George said. Like all he was doing here was *tinkering*.

It was wild, mad, and possibly a little insane.

Or maybe it was just a symptom of being drenched in magic for many, many years.

"Not just a tinkerer," Aidan defended staunchly.

Dexter smiled. Aidan might claim that he would never get over missing Tír na nÓg, but he was making friends and creating a place here for himself, day by day, week by week.

In a few years, he wouldn't even give Tír na nÓg a passing thought.

He couldn't see it, but Dex, who knew him inside and out, could.

"They are not quick to build," George said, "but I was just finishing this one over here, hoping to give it to Billy and Finn for a housewarming gift, at the beginning of the year. I'd be honored if you'd assist me."

"Me?" Dexter was surprised. "I'm not . . ."

"I hear you fixed the sleigh. You're obviously talented," George disagreed. "And besides, I can tell how much you're dying to get your hands on one."

Dexter shot George a sheepish grin. "Is it that obvious?"

George patted him on the shoulder with one gnarled, strong-looking hand. "Not to everyone, but to me, yes. Because we both like to know how things work."

"You should," Aidan encouraged him. "We have some time."

"Alright, twist my arm," Dex conceded.

"Come over here," George said, using his cane to walk over to a far worktable. There, what looked like the beginnings of a snow globe sat. The globe was separate from the base, and he'd begun to fashion the figures.

Dex recognized the familiar edifice of Billy's bakery and the base structure of one of the cottages that he'd seen dotting the frozen plain. There were two figures, just the barest outlines now, and George picked one of them up, using a tiny metal tool that he'd pulled from his leather apron to make small, minute adjustments to his appearance, carefully beginning to carve away some extra of the modeling clay, and slowly but surely Billy's distinct face began to emerge.

"You're an artist, not just a tinkerer," Dex said slowly.

"And you're an engineer, you're going to want to take a look at this base," George said with a glimmer of a smile on his face as he poked the metal tool in the direction of the unused base. "It's been giving me a little bit of trouble. Pull up a stool and see if you can figure out how to get the glow to emit consistently. It's been flickering all over the place. I'm worried there's a shoddy connection someplace."

Before the sleigh, Dex might have demurred because it was new technology to him. But he'd figured out the sleigh, hadn't he?

So he did just as George suggested and pulled up one of the sturdy wooden three-legged stools, and tugged a small box of tools closer to his right arm, turning over the snow globe base and beginning to identify the different parts and not only how they worked, but how they worked together.

He didn't know how much time had passed, but it must have been a while, because at some point, he glanced up and Aidan was sitting on the table next to him, munching away on one of Billy's cookies.

"Having fun?" Aidan said, a smile tugging up one side of his mouth.

Shit, he'd gotten totally lost in the work.

The mechanism of the snow globe was a beautiful one, streamlined and efficient, but also full of imagination and whimsy. It was the kind of thing that Dex would have been thrilled to create.

George had been self-deprecating, but Dex had a feeling that he was responsible for the elegant design.

"Sorry," Dexter said, not feeling very sorry at all, because it was honestly an honor to be allowed to tinker with it. But he was supposed to be spending this time with Aidan.

"Don't apologize," Aidan said, waving his hand, getting crumbs everywhere, which Dex surreptitiously brushed to the floor before George could see them. "You're really enjoying yourself, and to be honest, I'm really enjoying watching you."

"Really?"

But then Dexter remembered how much he'd enjoyed watching Aidan work when they'd been on the sleigh with Santa.

"Yeah," Aidan said warmly.

"How is it going, my young friend?" George asked, appearing over Aidan's shoulder. "Did you figure out what was missing?"

"Yes, I think so," Dex said, using a tool to show him how one of the connections was loose, that was likely causing the flickering that George had complained about.

"Brilliant," George said. "I'd have fussed with that for days."

Dexter had a feeling he was being nice, but he appreciated it, anyway.

"What's brilliant is this design," Dexter said. "I have to ask . . . you didn't have any say in the sleigh design, did you? Because I recognize some of the same concepts. Smaller, of course, and without the engine powering it, but it does feel similar."

George smiled. "I did have a say in it, to be honest. That was a long time ago. I'm sure it's been improved and changed quite a bit since I worked on it."

"Not as much as you'd imagine. A solid design doesn't need much tweaking," Dexter said, honored and pleased that Aidan had thought to bring him here, to introduce him to George.

He must have realized that George was a kindred spirit.

It made Dex love him even more.

And that was really what this was, wasn't it?

Love.

Well, shit, a corner of Dex's mind screamed, that's inconvenient.

Or the most inevitable thing in the world, his heart answered.

"You're a flatterer, but I'll take it because you're young and clever and make me feel a little of both again," George said with satisfaction. "Here," he said, setting a globe in front of Dexter. "I saw the way you were eying this one, and I thought, why not make a few quick adjustments, give you something to take back to help you remember your time here."

It was the snow globe with the cityscape scene, the one that had brought to mind so strongly his encounter with Aidan and Santa and the sleigh. But instead of the reindeer, now the sleigh resembled the one that Sam flew now, without the reindeer, and with its elongated engine compartment. And in addition, George had taken a moment to slightly alter the elf beside Santa, and now Dex recognized Aidan.

And next to Aidan was a figure of himself, in his army-green jacket, and wearing the wild smile he more felt than remembered.

Dex touched the glowing glass, and to his surprise, the snow began to fall inside, bringing the scene to life.

"Thank you," he said, because there were no real words for how precious this was. "I'll . . . I will cherish this, forever."

"Good," George said, clearing his throat. "Now you two better get a move on, get ready for the big gala."

Aidan glanced over at Dex and he was flushing again.

"Yes, we do definitely need to get to the gala," Dex said, grinning. He picked up the snow globe, cradling it like the precious thing it was in the curve of his arm. "You ready to go, Aidan?"

"Never been more ready," Aidan said, and they said their goodbyes and headed out of the snow globe workshop to the snowy wonderland outside.

Chapter Nine

"You sure you aren't going to get in trouble for skipping the gala?" Dex asked, as they passed group after group of elves, all dressed in their best Christmas finery. At least he had to assume that was finery, for elves. It was certainly bright and sparkly, though in the same red-and-green vein as before.

"I don't care if I do," Aidan said. "After all, you said it. I'm now the Elf Who Officially Saved Christmas. And you helped. What are they going to do to me? Kick me out?"

Dex shrugged. He was on edge, in all kinds of good ways. Itching, because despite his hesitation, he couldn't wait to get Aidan alone.

It had been an incredible morning and afternoon, but he was ready to move their celebration to a more private venue.

"Also," Aidan said, turning to him with a wild grin, "I'd almost guess that you *want* to go to shake everyone's hands at the gala instead of spending the time with me. Alone."

"You caught me, I'm addicted to uncomfortable small talk with elves," Dex teased.

The smile that lit up Aidan's face and his beautiful green eyes made all of this—and every single bit of what was to come—worth it.

"Come on, then, let's make awkward small talk in my room," Aidan said.

They stopped in front of a large building and Aidan entered a code into the keypad by the front door.

"Security?" Dex asked, surprised as the door swung open, letting them in.

Aidan rolled his eyes. "I still haven't figured out why Edmund insisted on it. He couldn't even explain it."

"Huh," Dexter said, as they headed through the festooned and decorated entryway, towards a long winding wooden staircase.

"So, everyone who's single or who hasn't earned one of the cottages, they stay in one of these buildings," Aidan said as they climbed the stairs. "There's four of them."

"I'm surprised they didn't try to give you a cottage because you're the bigwig elf," Dex pointed out after they reached the third level.

"Oh, they did," Aidan said. Dex was following him down a long corridor. Even here was draped in holly garlands with poinsettias dotting the corners. "But Edmund intervened, said I needed a more 'authentic' North Pole experience, whatever that means. Honestly, I was glad. I was already being singled out so much, it made me uncomfortable."

"Being given things you don't deserve?" Dex said. "I know all about that."

Aidan shot him a sympathetic look. "Your parents?" he asked.

Dexter nodded. "They're still so angry and frustrated and confused that I won't touch my trust. I told them I don't want it, that I never earned a penny of it. They don't get why I'm working. When I could just go to school and have plenty of money left over."

"They don't seem to know you very well," Aidan said slowly. Like he was worried he'd overstepped.

But it was exactly right. His parents had never seemed to know him very well. They'd definitely never known what to do with him.

"They don't. They never have. I . . . I keep hoping that will change, but maybe it never will."

"I'm sorry, Dex," Aidan said, but Dex shrugged. He was trying to make his peace with it, but it wasn't always easy.

Finally, they stopped in front of a door. He punched in another code, and then he pushed the door open.

It was a few simple rooms—living room with a couch and a chair, with an honest-to-God television, and in one corner, a desk with a tablet computer on top of it. A kitchenette stood in the other corner, with a few clean dishes piled on a rack next to the sink.

There were two doors, on the far side, which Dexter assumed led to Aidan's bedroom and the bathroom.

"It looks . . . shockingly just like my apartment," Dexter said.

"Really?" Aidan's mouth twitched. "It's not . . . it's not as clean as it could be."

Dex didn't know how it could be any cleaner. Sure, there was a sweater thrown across the back of the chair, and a few dishes piled on the counter, but otherwise it was fairly neat.

Of course, they might get to the bedroom—finally—and Dexter might discover that it looked like a hurricane hit it.

The bedroom.

Dexter swallowed hard. He didn't want to be nervous, but he was, kind of. The kissing had been great. Everything else was sure to be great too, but what if it was . . . too great?

You're overthinking this again, Dex's heart reminded him.

"Well, I like it, a lot. It looks like, well, it looks like you," Dex said with a smile.

Aidan blushed again. "Thanks."

Dex set the snow globe down on the coffee table in front of the couch. "I want you to show me where you write me all your emails? On the desk over there?" He pointed to the little makeshift desk.

"Yeah," Aidan said. He was still shifting his weight, not quite looking at Dex in the eye.

Like he was nervous, too.

The last thing Dex wanted was for Aidan to feel anything except maybe a nervous anticipatory excitement.

"Let me see," Dex said, leaning against the wall that separated the living room from the kitchenette and where the desk stood.

Aidan shot him a look that said, *really?* But he went over anyway, sitting down. "I thought you had a good imagination," he teased. "But here's the full look, just in case you wanted to save it for . . . later."

"Oh, you mean when I'm alone and thinking about you?" Dex said, raising an eyebrow. "I absolutely plan on remembering every minute of this for later, especially this particular view."

"Even this?" Aidan leaned back in an exaggerated movement. Dexter didn't miss how his tunic rode up, exposing a tiny strip of skin and his fingers itched with the need to not just look, but touch.

"Definitely this." Dexter pushed off the wall and came closer. Almost close enough to touch.

The light green of Aidan's eyes darkened. "Why don't you come over and see what else I thought about?"

Dexter swallowed hard. He was pretty sure he'd see the outline of Aidan's cock in those leggings.

He wanted to look, was nearly desperate to look, but he also *cared* a lot, and he wanted to do this right. Not do this only because it might be the only chance they'd ever get.

"Only if you're sure," Dex said.

Aidan's expression morphed from hunger to disbelief. "Really? You don't think I'm sure?"

"I don't know, but I need to know before we do anything more than kiss," Dexter said, hating how serious he sounded, but not knowing any other way than to be a hundred percent clear.

Aidan looked at him straight in the eye. "I'm sure, I've never been surer of anything in my whole life," he said.

It was all that Dex needed to take those few steps closer, and to wrap a hand around Aidan's neck, tilting him back for a hungry kiss.

Aidan gasped into his mouth, and even though they're done this a few times now, each time felt better than the last—and this particular kiss? It was wild and ravenous almost immediately, like they'd both been holding back.

Dex knew he had been. Hadn't been sure about Aidan, but from the way his hands were everywhere, touching and caressing and starting at his chest, his shoulders, and working their way down to his stomach, making anticipation build hot and heavy as one hand gripped a thigh, his tongue delving deeply into his mouth.

Aidan pulled back a fraction, breathing heavily. "I think . . . I think we should head to the bedroom."

"You . . . you've done this before, right?" It was fine if he hadn't, but if he was inexperienced, then Dexter wanted to know.

Aidan shot him another look. "I should be asking *you* this question. After all, you're the spring chicken. I'm sixty-eight years old. I've definitely done this before."

"Oh. *Oh.*" Dexter rocked back on his heels. He'd forgotten; it was tough sometimes to remember that even though Aidan looked young, he *wasn't* young.

"That's right," Aidan said smugly, and stood, and yeah, that was definitely the hard line of his cock in those leggings. The ones that Dexter had barely been able to tear his eyes off of more than once.

The first time he'd ever seen him, when Aidan had gone flouncing down one of the aisles, his tunic riding up slightly, he'd seen the clear outline of his ass in those tight leggings, and Dexter had, despite only knowing him for five minutes, wanted to bite it like a ripe peach.

At the time, he'd thought he was a dirty old man—until he'd discovered if anyone was the dirty old man in this scenario, it was Aidan.

Mind-blowing.

And, if Dex had anything to say about it, Aidan was a *little* smug about it.

Dexter reached for the hem of his t-shirt and tugged it over his head.

―⸺―

Aidan was already having trouble thinking straight.

The kiss they'd just shared had been so passionate and felt so goddamned right.

He was hard and aching, somehow even more because he knew Dex had seen.

And then, Dex, not content to just stand there, cool and calm and way too collected, had pulled off his shirt.

His chest was a chiseled expanse of pale muscle, with a trail of dark hair leading into his jeans.

Aidan's mouth watered and his breath hitched.

"That's not playing fair," Aidan complained, even though he could *hardly* complain about the way Dex looked.

He'd thought he was the hottest thing he'd ever seen, the first night they'd met.

And that had been a fully clothed Dex.

They'd already been playing with fire.

A shirtless Dex was a whole different kind of incendiary, and the sight in front of him was setting him alight.

"Oh?" Dexter raised an eyebrow, and he was so unbearably handsome and so dear that Aidan's heart clenched.

"Come on," Aidan said, reaching out and taking his hand. "Let's go to bed."

He'd had no idea this morning when he'd left his apartment that he'd be bringing Dexter home with him.

But Aidan still liked things neat. The bed was made, with its knit coverlet, in various shades of green, something he'd been allowed to bring with him from Tír na nÓg.

"Neat and tidy," Dex teased, and Aidan decided there'd been just enough teasing for today.

He already felt dangerously close to the edge, and he didn't know what would happen if Dex pushed him any further.

Giving Dexter a light shove, he went down onto the edge of the bed, and deciding his sixty-eight-year-old knees could handle this just fine, Aidan kneeled at his feet.

"What are you . . ." Dex said, but his words trailed off, wide shock and pleasure lighting up his face when Aidan pressed a palm against the erection in his jeans.

But Aidan had no intention of stopping there.

It'd been too long since he'd gotten to enjoy this and it felt like he'd only wanted Dexter forever—even though it had only been a year.

He popped open the button on Dex's jeans, and then pulled down the zipper, Dex leaning back, the flex in his arms sending another pulse of arousal through Aidan.

He made quick work of Dex's sneakers and his socks, and then pulled down his jeans, and then his underwear, freeing a long, hard erection that made Aidan lick his lips.

"Like what you see?" There was still that thread of smug amusement in Dex's voice, and Aidan didn't waste a moment. Just leaned forward and gave it a long lick, from base to tip, wrapping his tongue around the head and feeling it twitch.

"Fuck," Dexter swore, his long, drawn-out groan giving Aidan more motivation.

He wanted to make his man scream and he had the confidence to know he absolutely could.

And even better, all the elves would be at the gala and nobody would be any the wiser.

Aidan began a slow, teasing rhythm, sucking every third or fourth twist of his fingers around the base, just savoring the taste of Dex's cock on his tongue. He'd imagined this so many times, lying in this very bed, dreaming about a time in the faraway future when he might get to enjoy the man he loved like this, but the reality was better than any fantasy.

Dex kept begging, and when Aidan glanced up, saw that his arms were fully flexed, fingers dug into the covers, an agonized, overwhelmed expression on his face as Aidan worked him over with every ounce of his expertise.

Aidan let the spit-slick cock slide out of his mouth. "Like that, huh?" he teased. Was rewarded with a particularly fraught groan out of Dex. "I thought you might."

"You're way too fucking good at this," Dex ground out.

Aidan wasn't stupid enough to believe that a really great blowjob would convince Dex to stay here, with him, if he asked. But it sure wouldn't hurt.

And even if he wouldn't, even if he couldn't, he knew this was something he'd never forget—and he selfishly wanted Dex to always look back on this with pleasure.

So he redoubled his efforts. Dex was long and thick, and his jaw was aching but he took even more of him in, sucking hard on the head, and feeling the length of him twitch. Aidan cupped his balls, rolling them between his fingers with his other hand and was rewarded by feeling them tighten up.

"I'm . . ." Dexter said, voice garbled, but Aidan already knew he was about to come, and pushed himself that little bit further, letting Dexter pulse and explode down his throat.

He swallowed once, and then twice, loving the way Dexter kept groaning through it, like it was the best thing he'd ever felt.

When it was finally over, he rocked back on his heels, wiping the back of his mouth with his hand, not surprised to see his fingers trembling. He was so aroused that it wouldn't take more than a few strokes to make him explode.

Dex's eyes slowly fluttered open and the expression in them was worth every second. There was still a quiet lust in them, but it was more than that in their dark depths. There was care and affection and longing too.

Like no matter how much alone time they might steal, it wouldn't be enough for him.

Aidan already knew it wouldn't be enough for him.

He was going to want Dexter every day of his life.

"Come here," Dexter said gruffly, and Aidan pulled off his tunic, shed his leggings, and went into Dex's embrace willingly and gladly. Let Dexter wrap a hand around his aching cock, and as they kissed and kissed, Dexter used one of those capable, callous-roughened hands to draw out the kind of pleasure that Aidan didn't think he'd ever experienced in his life.

It was so good that even after it was over, and he sat, panting, in Dexter's lap, he could still feel the echo of it in his bones.

And in his heart.

Something that felt so goddamned good shouldn't sting so much.

They cleaned up and then Aidan pulled the coverlet back and spread himself out across Dex's much bigger, naked body.

"I almost," Dex said in a sleepy voice, "want to know how you learned to suck cock like that, but then I might get jealous."

"Really?" Aidan had never felt a hint of jealousy or even envy from Dex before, but they'd only exchanged emails, hadn't they? It might be hard to discern those emotions from words and text.

"No, not really, but maybe," Dexter said with a low chuckle. "Seriously, it was amazing."

This is it, Aidan's heart said with a hopeful clench, this is the moment you need to lay it all out on the line.

"I think . . . I think you might've been right," Aidan said.

"That it was a really good blowjob? Trust me, it was. Just about blew my head clean off."

"No," Aidan said. He felt so nervous, his throat was drying up. He swallowed hard. "Not that, though thank you, that's a compliment."

"So, what am I so right about?" Dexter wondered, his arm, slung around Aidan's back, tightening just a little.

"That I was really the Christmas Savior," he said. "And if I really was, if I actually did save Christmas, then maybe I could ask for something. For anything I wanted."

"Yeah, you could get one of those cottages, maybe," Dexter said.

The only reason he'd want one was if he was going to share it with Dexter. Aidan took a deep breath.

"I could ask for something bigger, even. Like . . . for a special dispensation. For you."

"For me?" Dexter sounded confused. Aidan wanted to swear. Why didn't he figure out exactly where he was going with this and put him out of his misery?

"For you, to . . . to come here."

"To visit?" Dex sounded excited now. "I'd love that."

"I don't know if that would be something they'd allow . . . but they might allow you to come here." Aidan felt his heart clench. "Permanently. To be with me."

Aidan felt Dexter tense underneath him, every muscle going on high alert.

"Is that . . . something you'd want?" Dexter's voice was careful. Too careful. And instead of answering Aidan's question, he'd asked another one.

"It is, of course it is." Aidan told himself to lay it all out there on the line. "I know we've only spent a little time together, but I know you. You know me. Better than anyone else does. More than anyone else has ever cared to. And . . . and I love you."

If Dexter had tensed before, he froze now.

Aidan didn't want to move, didn't want to see the expression on Dexter's face, but he didn't get a choice, because Dex was moving him, carefully, shifting him to the side so he could look him square in the eye.

"You really mean that," Dex said softly. The look in his dark eyes was agonizing. Or promising. Aidan didn't know.

And maybe Dexter didn't know either.

"You don't have to make a decision right now or anything," Aidan said quickly. "I . . . I don't want to rush you. I know it's a lot."

"I'd have to give up everything. My life. My friends. My career possibilities."

"You could always work here, there's so much you could do. Think of George, and what he's done. He worked on the sleigh, and now he creates those incredible snow globes."

"That's why you took me there," Dex said. His voice wasn't accusatory, but there was an edge of something there. "You've been thinking about this for awhile. Before Christmas Eve."

"Yes," Aidan said. Telling himself firmly that he was not pathetic.

No, he was merely in love.

Wildly, crazily, head over heels in love.

That was all.

It would be impossible to miss that Dexter still had not addressed that particular confession.

"Wow . . ." Dexter trailed off, scrubbing a hand across his jaw, his face. "I don't know what to say. I mean . . . obviously, I . . ."

Aidan waited, not very patiently, for him to say the words he was dying to hear.

But instead, Dex didn't finish the sentence the way he'd started it.

"It's just a lot," he said. "I need to think about it."

Aidan was miserable. This was going to ruin their last few hours together, but he couldn't help himself. "You don't feel the same way about me that I feel about you."

"No, no, *no*." Dexter's voice, hesitant before was strong and confident now. *Sure.* He took Aidan's jaw and cradled his face in his hand. "I care about you so much. I . . . I think I could love you. That I *do* love you. I've just never been in love before, I don't want to say it and not mean it, and I don't want to come here and ever have either of us regret it. Do you understand?"

Aidan did, even if he didn't want to. He nodded, swallowing back the mixture of hope and sadness and fear that had suddenly collected in his throat.

"Hey, don't look at me like that," Dexter said, and leaned in, kissing him gently on the lips, pressing his fingers against the coin still lying on his chest. "I'm crazy about you, you know that. You can *feel* that, I know you can."

"It's a lot," Aidan acknowledged, after he'd let the kiss drag on and on. It wasn't like he could use their clear sexual compatibility to convince him, but if this was all he was ever going to get of Dex, he wanted it all.

"That's all I'm saying," Dexter said. "Just . . . I need some time to think about it. That's all. I want to be sure."

"I want you to be sure, too."

He also, selfishly, wanted him to be sure *right now*.

Even if that was unfair.

"So," Dex said, putting on a forced cheerful edge to his voice. Trying, Aidan knew, to change the subject. Aidan had already decided to let him. "What else in the North Pole do I have to experience before I go?"

Aidan let the *before I go* statement resonate inside for little bit, feeling the inevitable sadness of it, before he pushed it aside. He wasn't going to ruin the last bit of time they had left by pouting and being miserable.

"I think . . . I think we need to cuddle and drink hot cocoa and watch your favorite Christmas movie."

Dex smiled soft and sweet. "Do you know what it is?"

"You've never said, but I have a few guesses," Aidan said solemnly.

"What's yours?"

"*Arthur Christmas*, of course."

"Of course," Dex said, lightly smacking himself on the forehead. "I should have guessed."

"It's just . . . nice. They get a lot of things wrong. We don't fly a spaceship, though we have embraced technology. And Edmund doesn't look much like Steve, but sometimes it's hard to miss the resemblance."

"And it has someone who doesn't fit in, who ends up saving Christmas," Dex teased.

"Right," Aidan said, telling himself that he shouldn't be so embarrassed at how transparent he was. Especially not with Dex. But he felt the flush of it anyway.

Maybe it would have felt different if Dex hadn't told him he'd have to think about it. If he'd been as sure as Aidan that this was love.

Aidan pushed the thought away again, shut it behind a door, locked it, and flipped the deadbolt.

"We could always watch *Arthur Christmas*," Dex said lightly. "I like that one, too."

"But it's not your favorite," Aidan said staunchly.

"Nope," Dexter said with a grin. "You going to tell me your guess?"

"I'm going to go with *The Santa Clause*, for a few reasons. First, that was the movie version you first asked me to compare the real North Pole to. And second . . . it's about family. Specifically about a father and a son."

Dex's eyes grew somber.

If he *knew* Aidan, better than anyone else, then the opposite was also true.

"You're good," Dexter said, sighing, pulling Aidan close again, letting his fingertips drift down his skin, an almost unconscious caress.

"I paid attention." He'd done a lot more than that.

"I gathered. So hot cocoa? Is that another North Pole tradition? What if I liked apple cider better?"

"Then," Aidan pointed out, "you'd better go find a Stonehenge elf to cuddle up to, because that's an All Hallows' Eve specialty. Hot cocoa is for Christmas."

"I didn't realize there were so many rules," Dex teased, fingertips lightly tapping along Aidan's upper arm.

"Gotta be rules, or else there's chaos," Aidan said, nuzzling in closer.

"Hot cocoa it is, then. With extra marshmallows, I assume." Dex sat up and Aidan nearly protested his loss, but then it *had* been his idea. Cuddle on the couch with hot cocoa and Dex's favorite Christmas movie. Surely that would be a lasting memory that he wouldn't forget anytime soon.

Aidan hoped he wouldn't be forgetting any of this, anytime soon.

"Extra marshmallows is how it *should* be served," Aidan insisted. "Besides, I picked up a big batch from Emmett at the candy shop two days ago, so not only will there be extra, they'll be fresh *and* homemade. Not like those plastic-tasting things from the store."

Aidan pressed a single kiss against Dex's cheek, and then slid out of bed, scrounging for his discarded clothes, before Dex could tempt him to stay.

―⁂―

Dex sat with Aidan on the couch, arm around his shoulders, a cup of steaming hot cocoa at his elbow, full of melting marshmallows, and pretended to watch *The Santa Clause*.

Aidan hadn't been wrong. It *was* his favorite Christmas movie, but now, he wasn't sure anything else would quite live up to the reality of the North Pole.

Or, he couldn't help but mentally add, the cold-water reality check of Aidan's offer.

Could he move here and abandon everything he knew and be happy?

You've already told yourself that you won't be happy without *him*, a voice inside him taunted, so how is this any different? Did you actually think an elf, the Christmas Savior, would ever be able to leave the North Pole to be with you?

Truthfully, he hadn't really thought about it.

In the hazy future of his dreams, he hadn't really placed them any specific place. The only concrete nonnegotiable had been that they were together. Together, and in love.

He'd already expected that to follow whatever job offer piqued his interest, he'd have to leave Chicago. At the time, he hadn't even seen it as a loss.

He and his parents were never going to see eye to eye, he knew that much. But it was a different thing entirely to remove completely the chance that they could ever reconcile. That they'd ever see the error of their ways and reach out and bridge the gap between them.

If he moved to the North Pole, there'd be no chance of that.

He'd have to do what Aidan did, and find a new family, here.

And he was even more different than Aidan was, he was a human, he wasn't ever meant to be here, and he'd probably feel the ache of the difference even more profoundly than Aidan had.

Of course, he'd have Aidan.

That was a huge plus for the pro column—maybe the only one that mattered, Dex thought morosely—but what about the cons?

He couldn't just dismiss them.

"You're quiet," Aidan said, murmuring into his shoulder.

Dex didn't know just how much time they had left. But however long it was, he already knew it wasn't going to be long enough.

"Just sleepy and happy," Dex answered honestly.

He'd never been so happy—and so torn—in his whole life.

It would be stupidity heaped on stupidity to turn his back on this, even if it was wrapped in packaging that he didn't quite recognize, that he wasn't entirely comfortable with.

He'd have *Aidan*.

Forever.

There'd be good, imaginative, unique, and interesting work for him to do, and maybe even a mentor in George.

He'd never be bored.

But he might never ever feel like he belonged, either.

It was something he'd taken for granted for every single one of his twenty-five years, something he'd barely even recognized, until the possibility occurred that he might lose it and never find it again.

"I'm happy too," Aidan said softly.

He hadn't meant it to hurt. Dex knew that. Aidan didn't have a cruel bone in his body. But his words struck with a double edge—the highest highs followed by the lowest lows.

The movie ended, and for a few minutes, neither of them moved.

Until, like clockwork, Aidan's communication device, that he'd carelessly tossed on the coffee table, next to Dex's snow globe, dinged.

And then dinged again.

And a third time.

"Shit," Aidan muttered under his breath as he untangled himself from Dex's embrace.

Dex let him go, even though he didn't want to.

He had a feeling that real life had again come calling.

From the way Aidan's expression morphed from frustration at being interrupted to an abrupt sadness, which filtered into resignation, Dex knew what was happening.

"It's time for you to go," Aidan said, turning so his face was shadowed. Like he didn't want to let Dexter see any of his pain at the inevitable. "We'd better get dressed. Sam said to meet him at the sleigh warehouse. He's going to transport us with magic."

"Okay," Dexter said. He almost said, *it's not goodbye forever, it's just goodbye for now*, but he didn't know if that was really the truth or not.

And if he didn't know, if he wasn't one hundred percent sure, it would be worse to offer a false promise. Both to Aidan and to himself.

Chapter Ten

They got dressed in the quiet of Aidan's apartment, and then after grabbing Dex's snow globe, headed out. The village was colder, but equally as quiet. Everyone else, it seemed, had finally gone to bed.

Sam was stomping his feet and warming his hands just outside the warehouse door.

"Good evening," he said solemnly. "I trust you two had a nice time?"

"It was wonderful," Dex spoke up, before Aidan could. Wanted to make sure that he didn't think Dex hadn't enjoyed every single moment of it.

"I hoped you would enjoy it up here," Sam said, gaze taking in the setting sun. "There's a bit of time left, so you can stay for a few minutes, when you get to Chicago," he said.

"You're sending me too?" Aidan sounded surprised.

Dex knew *he* was surprised. He'd been expecting that Sam would send just him back.

"I think I've got enough magic left in the tank to do it," Sam said with a small smile. "And besides, that's what you really wanted for Christmas, isn't it? To see where Dexter lives. To be there, with him."

Dex looked over at Aidan, and even though it was cold and they were bundled up, it was impossible to miss the flush that crested over his fair cheeks.

"Yes," he said. "That's what I asked for."

"Then you shall receive it," Sam said.

"How long will he have?" Dex discovered that now that there was a clock, counting down, he wanted it gone. Wanted to have more time, and then more again.

"An hour," Sam said softly.

It wasn't much, but it would have to be enough.

Dex nodded and took Aidan's hand, squeezing it. "We're ready," he said.

He hadn't known what magical transport would feel like, if it would feel more like crossing the magical barrier into the North Pole or if it would feel worse, maybe even nauseating like how apparating had been described in the *Harry Potter* books.

It turned out that it felt like neither.

Not the glowy, sparkling energy of the barrier, and not the pitch and roll of how he'd always imagined apparating would feel.

Instead, it felt warm and soft, comforting, almost, like he'd just been wrapped in a big sweater or a cozy blanket. His eyes closed, like he could fall asleep, and then he felt a *whoosh,* and when he opened them again, they were in his apartment in Chicago.

Aidan was smiling, that little bit of sadness that had lurked in his expression vanishing, finally.

"Wow," he said, turning around, taking in everything. "I'm really here, in your place."

"Now you know how I felt, just a few hours ago," Dex teased.

"And you were right," Aidan said, eyes wide, as he looked around, taking in everything from the worn couch to the desk in the corner to the scrubbed-clean kitchenette. "It *is* a lot like my place."

"Yours is a lot homier," Dexter said, pulling off his jacket and hanging it on the coatrack in the corner, right by the front door. Then he set the snow globe down, on the kitchenette countertop. "Mine's just . . . a place I'm keeping time, I guess."

Aidan shot him a knowing look. "I'm aware," he said dryly.

"What do you want to see?" Dex said, changing the subject again. He wasn't going to waste a moment of their last hour together rehashing this same argument.

He didn't know if it was the right thing for him to up and leave everything and move to the North Pole.

Even as he knew, without a doubt, that it was absolutely the right thing to do.

Maybe the argument, Dex thought with a dawning realization, wasn't even between him and Aidan—it was between the warring parts of himself.

"To be honest? I just want to see one thing. One place." Aidan sounded not only suddenly serious, but a little nervous too.

"What is it? I'll take you anywhere."

All Dexter got was a brief second of Aidan's eyelashes fluttering, before he was on the receiving end of a searing, hot-as-hell, sinful look. A look that promised more pleasure than he could stand. His cock hardened, surprisingly quickly, considering he'd only had sex a few hours before.

"Your bed," Aidan said, and reached up, pulling him into a hot, filthy kiss.

Aidan clearly wasn't done with Dex. And Dex wasn't done with him.

"I want you," Aidan murmured, lips only a millimeter from his own. "I want you to take me. To make me yours."

"Didn't I already?" Dex wondered.

Aidan's look was shy and yet full of heat. "I'd like more, if that's okay, if you'd be interested . . ."

Winding an arm around Aidan's waist, he tugged him even closer, letting him feel the beginnings of his arousal. "What do you think?" he teased softly.

"I just want to be clear about it," Aidan said, flushing again. "I don't know what the . . . methods are here. I don't want to do something you don't like, aren't comfortable with . . ."

Dex could hear the difference in Aidan's confidence from before, when they'd been at the North Pole and he'd taken over and taken control.

He leaned in, leaned down, brushing his mouth just over Aidan's ear, feeling him shudder with pleasure. "Are you asking if I'd like to fuck you or you'd like to fuck me?"

"Yes," Aidan said, swallowing hard.

Dex felt his own excitement rise higher and higher. He couldn't deny that he'd thought about this, that he'd *wanted* this.

"I guess, then, it's time for me to show you *my* bedroom," Dex said softly, and then Aidan reached up, capturing his mouth in a hot, passionate kiss.

Like it was everything that he couldn't say in words.

Aidan never looked like he weighed a thing—he was slender, and shorter, and so Dex took a chance and, sliding his hands around his glorious ass, boosted him up, and like he'd expected, it was easy enough to turn around and carry him into the bedroom.

Even if it hadn't been easy, Aidan's gasp and the way his kiss turned rough and eager would have made it worth the effort.

"Oh God," Aidan groaned as Dexter set him on the edge of the bed. "You're gonna ruin me, aren't you?"

"Ruin you?" Dexter grinned. He turned, grabbing supplies out of the bedside table. "I thought I was going to make you mine."

"I was wrong," Aidan said, leaning forward, punctuating each word with a single kiss. "I'm already yours."

His eyes glowed, the sheer happiness on his face taking Dex's breath away. "Are you?" he asked.

"You know I am," Aidan said, and that confidence was back as he reached out, palming Dex's erection with an expert motion that left him suddenly unsure that he could make this last, especially if Aidan kept touching him like that.

He swatted Aidan's hand away, reaching out and pulling his tunic over his head. Aidan already had his leggings down, and Dex leaned in, giving the head of his cock, already hard and leaking precome, a quick brief lick.

"Up," Dex ordered, and Aidan scrambled, moving up further onto the bed, spreading his legs like he'd been made for him.

And maybe he had been, Dex thought wildly, beginning to lose the hold he had over his self-control. He felt that good. He sounded that good. He was everything Dex had ever wanted— funny and kind and loyal, with a sweetness and a specialness that seemed to exude out of every pore.

Did it matter if he was an elf and he lived in the North Pole and Dex was a human and didn't?

Dex was no longer sure that it did.

Not when Aidan was opening up to him like his favorite gift.

"Please, more," Aidan pleaded as Dex wet his fingers with the lube he'd grabbed from the drawer.

Dex didn't need any more encouragement. He slid his thumb down, rubbing it across Aidan's hole, and lowered his head, sucking the head of his cock into his mouth.

Aidan's broken groan spurred him on, because he wanted to hear that more and more, until that was the only sound echoing in his head.

He slid a finger in, and then a second, working his cock, feeling it twitch against his tongue.

Aidan's groans and semi-coherent pleas bled into increasing gibberish, which Dex loved.

He would make his man moan, and he would make him scream, if he had anything to say about it. His own cock was pressing hard and uncomfortable against the fly of his jeans but he kept going, wanting to wring every bit of pleasure that he could from Aidan's body.

Wanting to show him just how goddamned special he was.

How much he wanted to do this.

How privileged he was that Aidan had asked for it.

Then, suddenly, Aidan sat up, and shot him a challenging look. "You're going to make me come," he said frankly, "and I don't want that, not until you're inside me."

"Are you . . ."

Aidan's glare was uncompromising.

Another reason he loved him.

Because he did, didn't he?

He really loved him.

Dex knew he had to tell him, but he couldn't do it now, in the middle of sex. Aidan might not believe he really meant it if he said it now.

But as he shed his clothes, it was still on the tip of his tongue. The only thing that kept him from saying it was Aidan's incendiary kiss as he climbed on top of him, condom in place, as he carefully slid into Aidan's willing and waiting body.

It was such a fucking cliche, but it was like coming home, being inside of Aidan.

It overwhelmed and it grounded him, all at the same time.

He felt remade as he began to thrust, and every sexual encounter he'd ever had before this one faded away, suddenly inconsequential.

This was how it felt to be with someone you really cared about. Someone you loved.

Dex felt it in the way his arms shook with the strain of going slowly, with not just wallowing in the glory of Aidan's tight passage, and the way Aidan's breath hitched, the way his hands clutched against Dex's shoulders. The way his eyes never left Dex's.

He had a feeling this was a first for both of them, and he wanted it to go on and on, and never end, but it was so good, so life-changing, the ecstasy racing through him like a freight train, inescapable and inevitable, that when Aidan clenched around him, moaning especially loudly, his fingers wrapping around his cock, working himself through his orgasm, it was impossible for Dex not to tumble headfirst into his own pleasure.

Aidan might be slight but he was strong. And Dex didn't worry about him as he collapsed onto him, trembling all over.

And because he was simply incredible, instead of just lying there, Aidan reached out and stroked his hair, once, and then again.

"That was . . ." Aidan hesitated, sounding flustered, overwhelmed.

Dex understood because the same feelings were coursing through him.

He didn't know how to explain them in words. Wouldn't even know where to begin. Was relieved that it wasn't just him who couldn't find the right ones.

"Yeah," Dexter said. "Yeah, it really was."

Finally he straightened and levered himself off Aidan. "Gonna get cleaned up," he said, pressing a kiss against Aidan's temple, damp with sweat. "Be right back."

The fluorescent light of the bathroom didn't jolt him back to reality. He felt permanently transported. Forever changed.

He hadn't fallen in love with Aidan right now. He'd been attracted to him immediately. Had wanted to *know* him. But it had happened so slowly, so gradually, that he hadn't even realized he was falling until he was sliding down that last little bit of slope, head over heels.

What he needed to do was go back into the bedroom and confess the truth. Tell Aidan that he would do whatever it took to make sure that they never lost each other.

Even if that meant Dexter giving up everything here, in Chicago, and moving to the North Pole.

He wouldn't be able to do it right away. Aidan might not understand, but he needed to finish out the last few months of his degree. Settle things here. Figure out what he was going to tell Jonathan, and maybe even his parents.

Dex finished cleaning up, disposing of the condom and wetting a washcloth, returning to the bedroom. Aidan was dozing in the bed, clearly worn out.

Dex leaned in, cleaning him up as best as he could, and tossing the dirty cloth into the laundry basket in the corner, climbed into the bed and pulled Aidan close. He'd known he was tired but it was only now, wrapped around the man he loved in his warm, comfortable bed that he felt the exhaustion begin to overwhelm him.

It had been a long day, but also the best day ever.

Memories filtered through his head, and each one better than the last, and with happiness suffusing him, he nodded off to sleep.

Aidan watched Dexter sleep.

He understood why Dex needed to be sure.

Understood why Dex wasn't quite ready to give up everything he knew.

If he'd had a choice about leaving everything he knew at Tír na nÓg and going to the North Pole, he might have demurred too. He'd at least have wanted to have the time to come to terms with the change on his own, to make the decision a reasoned and rational one.

He might have gone, in the end, but what convinced him once and for all that he couldn't push Dexter into this decision was his own experience.

He wished he'd had the room to make his own choice.

So, no matter how much it stung—and no joke, it hurt like hell to even *think* about leaving, and he was going to do more than just think about it—he was going to give Dexter the space to make the decision.

Aidan slid out of bed, ignoring the fierce way his heart was throbbing, and got dressed. He pressed one last kiss against Dexter's forehead, thinking of how much he flat-out loved him, and then went back into the living room.

There was a notebook on the desk.

Aidan pulled out a blank page and found a pen in the cup on the desk, and sat down to write, knowing he didn't have much more time before Sam came for him.

Dear Dex, he wrote,

I thought about waking you up and telling you this in person, but I think it might be too hard, so I'm not. Besides, I've said almost everything that matters to you in letters, so maybe this makes more sense.

I love you. I want you to come to live with me in the North Pole. That hasn't changed.

But I know how much of a change this will be for you. I know, because I did it too, and unlike how the decision was forced on me, I want you to decide to come to the North Pole because you can't see yourself anywhere else. Not because you feel obligated to be with me.

So I'm giving you the space to make that choice.

No matter what you decide, I'm always going to love you.

But until you make that choice, I think we should give each other some space. I don't trust myself to not beg you to come in every single email—and this is a decision you need to make for yourself.

But when you know, you know just where to reach me and how.

I'll miss talking with you more than just about anything, because in just a year, you've changed everything. But I wouldn't ever forgive myself if I was selfish and let you do something you didn't want to do—or that you weren't ready for.

Maybe that's what love is.

If it is, it kinda sucks.

Still wouldn't trade it for anything else in the whole world. You'll remain my most precious and most wonderful Christmas gift.

I hope you have a happy New Year, and that some time in it, I'll open my email and hear from you again.

Always yours,

Aidan

Aidan brushed a stray tear away and swallowing hard, he stood. Maybe it was cowardly to leave like this, after the experience they'd just shared, but he really thought if he didn't leave now, he would never want to leave at all.

He heard someone clear his throat behind him, and when he turned, Sam was standing there, a sympathetic expression on his kind face.

"It's the right choice," Sam said, as Aidan felt more tears begin to fall. "He's got to want it too, not just for you."

"I know, but . . ." Aidan knew he was about ten seconds away from just bawling hysterically. "We need to go. Now."

Sam didn't say anything else, and suddenly, they were flying and moving, and the next time Aidan opened his eyes, he was alone in his own room.

The first thing he saw was Dex's cup of half-drunk cocoa, and he burst into tears.

CHAPTER ELEVEN

Dex woke up the next morning, his phone alarm beeping insistently, and for a second he wasn't quite sure where he was.

When he reached out, his phone wasn't where he normally put it on the nightstand. Fumbling around some more, he finally concluded that he must have put it some other place.

Groaning, he rolled over, and froze.

The last day and the evening before came back to him in fits and starts.

Seeing Aidan again.

Kissing Aidan.

Helping Aidan fix the sleigh.

Then the incredible, whirlwind tour of the North Pole.

Dex scrubbed a hand over his face, over the prickly beard that had grown over the last day.

Somehow, he still wasn't sure when, he'd fallen in love.

But when he reached out, hoping to feel Aidan's warm body sleeping next to him, he already knew the spot that he already knew belonged to him would be cold.

Sam had been generous but clear—Aidan needed to return to the North Pole.

He must have done it while he was sleeping.

Why hadn't he woken him up to say goodbye?

Dex didn't need an answer, because he already knew why.

It was too hard.

He hadn't known how he would say goodbye to Aidan, and it was clear that Aidan had felt the exact same way.

What he wanted was to stay in bed and wallow, but his alarm was still going off and the walls in this apartment building were so thin that he'd start getting complaints if he didn't find his phone and turn off the beeping soon.

Groaning, he got out of bed and padded, still naked, out of the bedroom into the living room. Sure enough, his phone was still tucked in the pocket of his jacket.

He hadn't missed it, not once, when he'd been in the North Pole with Aidan.

Will you miss it when you go back? he wondered.

Because he knew, as strongly as he'd known anything in his life, that he would be going back.

Even if he could live without Aidan, he didn't want to.

After silencing the alarm, he saw a handful of messages from Jonathan.

Where you at? the first one read.

You still alive, bro? Dex chuckled when he read that one.

I hope you're not wallowing in your holiday misery, said the third.

Dex replied.

Wasn't wallowing. Was meeting up with my mystery guy.

Jonathan's response was almost immediate.

Was he as good as you hoped?

It wasn't hard to answer that. **Even better.**

At some point, despite how secretive the elves were, Dexter knew he was going to have to tell Jonathan.

Probably at some point before he disappeared into the North Pole.

He didn't know if Sam would ever let him return to the human world.

That was something he was going to have to figure out how to deal with.

He had five months left til graduation.

Five months to figure out if he was sure, and once he was, five months to tie up any loose ends.

It was December, so it was cold in his apartment—not as cold as it was in the North Pole, but he'd grown up here, so it probably wouldn't be too much of an adjustment in the end—so he headed back to the bedroom for clothes so he could find some breakfast.

Out of the corner of his eye he saw the ripped edge of a piece of paper sitting on the laptop on his makeshift desk.

At first, when he grabbed the letter, he'd been thrilled, excited that Aidan *had* said goodbye after all.

Then he read the letter.

And then read it again.

Then a third time.

Stood there, for a long time, fingers crinkling the edge of the paper.

He'd never imagined that for the next five months, he wouldn't have Aidan present in his life.

He'd become an integral thread in the fabric of it. Dex didn't know how to even *exist* if he couldn't wake up in the morning and check his inbox, hoping there'd be a note from Aidan.

If he couldn't tell Aidan about the things that happened with Mr. Husseini and the store. Or the latest terrible guy that Jonathan had met online.

It was like the age-old question: if a tree fell in the middle of the woods, would it make a sound?

If Dex couldn't relay all the minute details of his life, all the insignificant chaff that might not matter to anyone else, were they actually happening? Was he really living?

He wasn't sure.

The one thing he *was* sure of was that Aidan loved him.

Loved him enough to give him up so he could make the right choice.

It was impossible not to think of the way Aidan's choice had been made for him, and feel a pang in his heart at how Aidan hadn't wanted the same shitty situation for him.

No, to be the man that Aidan deserved—the man Aidan loved—Dex was going to have to follow suit and really give this decision consideration.

Give it the weight and importance it deserved.

It was the grownup thing to do.

But it also just really sucked.

Aidan,

I love you. I should have said it the moment I thought it.

I'd have a lot more regret, but I know, without a single doubt, that I will see you again, and that this time I'll say it, without hesitation.

Our time isn't over, it's just starting, but I still miss you.

I know it's unfair of me to send this. I know you said you wanted to give me space, so I could make the right choice for me (and for you), but not having you in my inbox every day is such a bummer. Not having you in my life is such a bummer.

I just miss you a lot. Think about you all the time. Hope you're doing good, and not letting Edmund boss you around too

much.
You're too amazing to take his shit.
Dex
(email deleted)

———ele———

Aidan,
I still fucking miss you.
That's all. That's the email.
Dex
(email in outbox, unsent)

———ele———

Aidan,
Less than a month of school left.
Mr. Husseini told me today that I seem "diminished."
He asked me if everything was okay.
Jonathan's asked at least a hundred times in the last few months. I wanted to tell him the truth, that I'm not okay, that I miss you like crazy, that I'm going nuts without you, but I didn't.
But I really, really wanted to.
Actually—scratch that. That's not true. The person I wanted to tell was you.
Dex
(email deleted)

———ele———

Two weeks of school left.
Jonathan keeps pestering me to go look at this place with him.

If he only knew I didn't actually take the job that the company here offered me. I got right up to the final interview and told them never mind.

I feel like I'm about to do something crazy, cashing out my trust fund, paying off my school loans, and giving the rest to Jonathan, and well . . . doing the inevitable . . . selling everything I own . . . moving to the North Pole . . . coming to see you.

(email never sent)

—ele—

Dex,

I wish you knew how much I missed you, though you probably know, because you're probably going through the same thing.

Giving you space to make the right choice is the hardest thing I've ever done, because I don't know what's going to happen.

I thought moving to the North Pole sucked, but actually, what really sucks is waiting for you to decide if you're coming too.

If you never decide, I may wait forever. Just putting that out there.

And elves, for the record, live for a really freaking long time.

You would too, if you moved here. The magic that gives us such long life would give you the same gift.

We could be together for many years to come.

It's hard, especially when I think about all the things I may never get to do with you. Everything that I'll never say.

But then I remember the look you gave me right before you fell asleep and I know, without a question, without a single doubt in my mind, that I'll see you again.

Aidan
(email deleted)

―⁓⁓―

"How are you doing, really?" Sam asked as he and Aidan sipped their hot cocoa.

He still couldn't drink it, couldn't unwrap marshmallows from Emmett's without feeling a pang of something painful in the vicinity of his chest.

It had been a few months since he'd left Dexter in bed, and he still thought about him about a million times a day.

He still hoped every day that he'd open his email and see an answer from Dex.

Some mornings he wanted it so much he could barely breathe, and some mornings, the bad mornings, he dreaded seeing Dex's reluctant, resigned message. That he'd moved on. That he'd decided against coming to the North Pole.

But instead, there'd been nothing but silence.

Which meant that there was still hope.

And Aidan lived for that hope.

Especially as the days and weeks ticked by. Whether he made a choice or not, Aidan had decided that he'd never leave Chicago before he finished his degree.

He'd worked too hard for it.

Dexter wouldn't abandon it nearly finished.

"I don't know," Aidan said. "I'm . . . I still think he's going to decide to come. I can't stop believing that he will. But some days are harder than others." He and Sam had grown closer after the whole incident with Dex, and to Aidan's surprise, Sam had started to seek him out more, and over the last few months, they'd formed a genuine, caring friendship.

Sam wasn't just a Santa, he was a person, with emotions and thoughts and feelings and his own kind of history.

"I should have done this before," Sam had confessed when they'd first started sharing cocoa a few times a week.

"Done what?" Aidan has asked, confused.

"Gotten to know you," Sam said, "but I didn't know what to make of you."

"It's okay," Aidan had admitted. "I don't think anyone did. I didn't know what to make of myself, at first, at the North Pole."

"But you don't hate it here anymore?" Sam had asked, and Aidan couldn't miss the hopeful edge in his voice.

"I don't think that I ever *hated* it, but yeah, it's growing on me. Kind of like a disease."

Sam had thrown his head back and laughed.

"I wanted to show you something today," Sam said, as they walked out onto the tundra. "Something that nobody else knows about."

Aidan raised an eyebrow. "Even Edmund?"

"Especially Edmund," Sam said with a knowing grin. "He wouldn't be able to handle it. I . . . I think you should know, though. Because you're integral to it."

"To what?" Sam was leading them towards a corner of the tundra, right near the patch of evergreens that lined one edge of the magical barrier. As far as Aidan knew, there was nothing out here except trees.

"To this," Sam said as they came to a clearing in the middle of the forest.

As they walked closer, Aidan could see that there was a pond, frozen over, but that it wasn't just any pond. It was glowing, bright blue and white, with the kind of magical energy that George used in his snow globes and that powered the sleigh's engine.

"What is it?" Aidan asked, walking closer, and then closer still.

"It's the wellspring of North Pole magic," Sam said. "And I know it seems bright now, but you should have seen it a hundred years ago. It lit up this entire forest."

"And it doesn't, not anymore?" Aidan guessed.

"No. Not for some time. Not enough humans believe anymore. And as you know, elf belief is not as strong, because it's easy to believe in something you can see, that is right in front of you every single day. But for humans . . ."

"They don't believe. Not always. Not anymore," Aidan guessed. He sat down heavily on a log.

"I show you this," Sam said, taking a seat next to him, "not to scare you, or to worry you, but because I believe, have always believed, that your role here was to not just save one Christmas but to save *all* Christmases."

Aidan gaped at him. "You don't think I was just supposed to help Dex fix the sleigh?"

Sam's eyes twinkled at him. "Do *you* believe that was all you were meant to do?"

"No," Aidan confessed. He still believed—and this coming from Sam now seemed to further encourage that belief—that Sam had engineered the entire sleigh breakdown in the first place.

But why?

"Because," Aidan confessed, suddenly realizing what it was that made him so special, "because I want to mingle our worlds. Because I fell in love with a human."

Sam nodded. "Dexter is part of this, of course, because he's the physical manifestation of your ability to see more in humans than other elves, but also the mingling of our worlds is key, I believe. We need to open ourselves up to the human world, and convince them to believe, again."

"Then why have you never told Edmund to fuck off?"

Sam, taking a drink of cocoa, choked as he laughed at Aidan's bluntness. "Because it's not just Edmund who believes that. And as much as you've discovered that I'm more, many elves see me as a symbol and nothing else."

"Santa," Aidan agreed with a nod, "and not Sam."

"That's right. But you? You're the Christmas Savior. There's no end of what you could do."

"What happens if Dex never decides to come?" Aidan hated how plaintive he sounded.

Sam shrugged. "Then he doesn't come. Your goals don't change. They didn't change because of Dex, did they? No, they only became more pronounced, your desire to see him helping you speak out. You enjoyed going into the human world before, when you lived at Tír na nÓg. That part of you has never changed, Aidan."

"I suppose . . ." Aidan considered it. How he'd been in the North Pole for several months before he'd ever met Dexter, and how Sam was right; he'd been feeling those same things, though perhaps not to the extent he had been over the last year, since the moment he'd arrived here.

"You're the catalyst of change," Sam said. "Dexter is important. But he's not the most important thing."

"You're saying that it's me." Aidan knew how hesitant he sounded. The mantle of Savior had never sat right on him. It had always felt too heavy of a burden, too random of a choice, for it to ever feel comfortable.

But maybe . . . maybe if he shared it.

Maybe he wasn't solely responsible for it.

Maybe if all he had to be was the spark and the oxygen that fanned the flames . . .

"That is what I'm saying," Sam said heavily. "I wasn't sure if I should tell you, especially with what you've been going through with Dexter, but I reminded myself that you're strong. You've got an incredible strength of will, Aidan."

"And I'm going to need it."

Sam chuckled under his breath. "Yes, I do believe you will."

"With or . . . without Dexter." It hurt to even think it. And Aidan hadn't given up hope. He wasn't sure he ever would.

Maybe that fierce hope and that fierce belief were what set him apart.

Made him the Christmas Savior.

Not some random star he'd been born under.

"You'll do it, I know you will," Sam said, giving him a firm, reassuring pat on his shoulder.

For the first time, Aidan really, truly believed.

And the pond began to glow a tiny bit brighter.

"I don't know what you're saying."

Dex hadn't really known *how* to tell Jonathan.

It was not going to be the easiest of conversations.

He hated to lie, but he also knew he couldn't tell the truth. He was too much of a pure engineer, and he'd want evidence, and all kinds of proof that Dex could never present.

There was the snow globe, the one that sat on Dexter's nightstand and the one he stared at every night, before he fell asleep. But that wasn't proof that the North Pole existed.

At first, he'd tried to keep a level head, trying to be impartial and telling himself that he hadn't *really* decided, that he was still making up his mind.

But after a month or so, it became impossible to pretend that he hadn't decided and he wasn't just marking time until he graduated and sent Aidan the email he was waiting for.

And then that morphed into a bigger, better, brighter idea that he wouldn't just send some impersonal email.

From what Sam and Aidan had told him, he could *go* to the North Pole, to the magical barrier. Maybe he couldn't enter it, not without the magical "key," but he could . . . knock?

That was the kind of epic romantic gesture he needed to give Aidan, to show he was sure.

Not some bloodless, spineless email.

He would sell everything, sign his trust over to Jonathan, and he would go to the North Pole.

Would it be easier if Sam magically transported him?

Yeah, but that would be *too* easy.

Aidan had done this incredibly hard thing, giving him the space he needed to make the decision. If Dex took the easy way out, it wouldn't show anything. It certainly wasn't going to prove his love.

The only difficulty left was . . . well, it was telling Jonathan.

He'd already written a letter for his parents, telling them he was being assigned to a secret government project at a remote location, and that he didn't expect to come back anytime soon.

They'd already lived without him for years. It hurt, but Dexter didn't think they'd miss him any more in the future than they did now.

He'd already found his new family.

Jonathan . . . well, he was the hardest part of his life to leave behind.

He knew Sam had made an exception for him, because of how he and Aidan felt about each other, but he wasn't stupid enough to believe that Sam might make another, for his best friend.

"I'm saying that I'm going away, for a long time. Maybe for years. Maybe forever."

Jonathan's forehead creased. "A secret government project? I didn't even know this was on your radar. You didn't tell me."

"I know, I couldn't," Dex confessed. His hot cocoa sat in front of him, untouched. He felt sick. He hated lying. But he didn't know what else to do.

Jonathan crossed his arms over his chest. "What about your mystery man?"

"Uh, well . . . he's part of this. The project that is."

"So you're going to take this job to be with him," Jonathan stated incredulously.

"Yeah, partly. But also because it's a great opportunity. The kind of opportunity I've been searching for all my life."

That was the truth. When he'd written his wish into the book, he'd wished for a new family, and even though he wasn't sure the North Pole would ever accept him, he'd met enough of them that he thought would. And his fingers had been itching to take apart the snow globe, to see how it really worked, to see if he could figure out how to make it run better, more efficiently. The only thing that had kept it intact was his fear that he wouldn't be able to get it to work right outside of the North Pole.

"I can't believe you'd give up everything you worked for, for a *guy*," Jonathan said.

"I'm not, it's . . . it's everything. It's the guy. It's the job. It's . . . honestly, it's a great chance for me. I know you're not happy . . ."

"No fucking joke, I'm not happy," Jonathan muttered. "You're my fucking best friend."

"You *are* my best friend, and I want you to be happy for *me*, if you can. We'll be able to email, and I'm sure I'll be back at some point." At least that was something that Dexter hoped.

"Oh, is that all?" A smile cracked through Jonathan's disgruntled expression. "You just want me to be happy for you?"

"That and . . ." Dex hesitated. "I want to sign my trust over to you."

"What?" Jonathan's jaw dropped. "What for?"

"Because I'm never going to need it or use it, and you could. Pay off your school loans." Dex had already paid off his. He had no intention of leaving any debt here. "Use it to get established somewhere. Buy a house or a condo or something. Blow it all on one of your shitty boyfriends."

"They're not *all* shitty," Jonathan said, but he was smiling. "Not every guy can be your amazing, fantastic, wonderful mystery guy."

"Aidan," Dexter said. "His name is Aidan."

"Only took a year and a half to find out his name. Well, here's the thing: I *am* happy for you. The trust thing, well, it's a lot. I don't know if I should take it."

"Why not?"

Jonathan shot him a look as he sipped his coffee. "*You* never took it."

"Not true. I didn't for a long time, but I did just use it to pay off my loans."

Jonathan looked surprised.

"You're really serious about this, aren't you? You're going to up and disappear and I'm going to see you probably a handful of times. And one day you're going to show up with your mystery guy, and you're going to be in trouble, like you're going to be tailed by some super secretive government spies or something."

Dex laughed so loud that a few of the other patrons of the coffee shop turned their heads in his direction. "No, no, I promise you that isn't going to happen."

Jonathan raised an eyebrow. "Well, let me live a little vicariously through you, okay?"

"Okay," Dex said. If that was what Jonathan wanted to believe, he'd let him.

"When are you leaving?" Jonathan asked.

"Next week." Graduation was in two days. He had a few other loose ends to tie up, but he was just about ready to leave, and with every day that passed, his excitement grew.

He couldn't wait to show up in the North Pole and see Aidan again.

―――⁂―――

Aidan was supposed to be helping Billy with the weekly cookie bake, but instead of scooping dough out onto trays, he was leaning against the counter, lost in thought.

"You going to actually work instead of moping?" Billy asked, his voice kind.

"Uh, yeah, sorry." He actually *hadn't* been moping, but Aidan supposed he couldn't really blame Billy for making the assumption. After all, it was a lot of what he'd been doing since Christmas, when he'd left Dexter in his apartment and hadn't heard from him since.

"It's alright," Billy said, giving him a smile. "I know you've been going through it. I always feel better when I'm working with my hands, creating something delicious. It's why I asked Edmund for your help this week."

Aidan enjoyed it too, which was why he hadn't complained much when Edmund had informed him two days ago that he'd be spending the next week with Billy in his bakery. "I don't know why he needs you this week in particular," Edmund had grumbled, but he hadn't protested all that much.

Not many of the elves understood why exactly that was, but Aidan did, because he knew Belinda had finally made a move on the perpetually disgruntled Head of Elves, and that behind closed doors, they were blissfully happy.

Edmund still put a show on, but it helped that Aidan knew the truth—that his bark was much worse than his bite. Belinda had officially slain the beast.

"It does help," Aidan agreed with Billy. "I'm glad you asked for me this week."

"Have you heard from him?" Billy asked. He was one of the few elves who actually knew why the Christmas Savior had been so quiet and withdrawn the last few months.

"No," Aidan said. Trying not to do what Billy had *just* accused him of and mope about it. "But I didn't really expect to, before his graduation anyway. He would have wanted to finish his degree."

"I didn't spend too much time with him," Billy said with a nod, "but I could see that would be important to him. Don't worry and don't give up hope, Aidan. He's going to come around."

"I hope so," Aidan said.

And he did, every single day.

The door to the bakery opened and George hobbled in, his breath coming in deep wheezes, his cane and his legs moving faster than Aidan had ever seen.

"Come quick," George said when he'd caught his breath.

Aidan—and Billy—stared.

"What's going on, George?" Billy asked, sounding concerned. "Is everything alright?" Billy had probably never seen George move that quick; Aidan knew he never had.

But George was staring not at Billy, but straight at Aidan, and that intense look stirred something deep inside of him. It wasn't just hope, because he'd lived with hope every day for the last five months. This was something more.

This was excitement.

Something had happened to finally break the doldrums that he'd lived with since leaving Dex.

"Aidan, you need to come quick," George said, ignoring Billy.

Aidan was already dropping the cookie scoop onto the countertop, and stripping his apron off as he dashed outside.

"At the edge of the barrier," George said breathlessly, pointing in the direction of the forest.

Aidan took off at a run. There were other elves streaming out of their houses, roused by George or someone else, but Aidan ignored them as his shoes slipped and slid across the frozen tundra.

His lungs were aching with the cold and the exercise by the time he reached the edge of the barrier, but he was barely aware of them.

He was aware of only one thing: there was a tall, dark-haired figure standing on the other side of the glowing blueish-white barrier, face obscured by the shimmer of the magic, but Aidan didn't need to see his face to know who it was.

Dexter was here; he had come for Aidan.

Come to be *with* Aidan.

Aidan didn't know whether to laugh or to cry. Of course the jerk couldn't be bothered to send something as simple and straightforward as an email.

No, he had to actually come to the freaking North Pole.

He forced his legs to run faster and faster until he skidded to a stop right in front of where Dex stood.

"Hello." He was close enough now that he could hear Dex's voice, faintly muffled by the hum of the magic, but then he was laughing *and* he was crying. He reached through the barrier, feeling the magic scrape along his skin, electrifying him, and then he felt the touch of Dexter's hand as it grasped his own, and that was electrifying in a completely different kind of way.

He was laughing, and he was crying, tears dripping down his cheeks.

Happiness? Relief? The sheer incredible force of love?

Maybe all of the above.

"Hi," Aidan said, and then tugged, pulling him through the barrier. Maybe he wasn't a Santa, but he still had echoes of Sam's magic running through him.

"I've been knocking on your front door for awhile," Dexter said, and his smile was brilliant.

"Sorry, I didn't hear it at first," Aidan said. His heart was galloping so fast he thought he might keel over.

"Can you hear me now?" Dex asked.

Aidan laughed. He couldn't help it. "Yes, I definitely can hear you."

"I wanted to make sure, because I'm only going to get to say this for the first time once and well . . . I should've told you before, because I felt it, but it scared the shit out of me." Dex took a deep breath. "I love you. I love you so much."

Aidan didn't know whether he was laughing. Or he was crying.

Maybe both.

"I love you too."

"Also, I thought I might stop by, see if the offer was still open," Dex said, his casual voice the direct opposite of the huge bag at his side, and the burning love in his eyes, "because I still want you, if you'll have me."

"I'll have you. Today. Tomorrow. For a hundred years." Aidan jumped into his arms, and they were suddenly kissing, and it was miraculously even better than it had been before.

Because now Aidan knew it was forever.

Epilogue

Christmas Eve

"Did you get the tool kit?" Edmund asked, his normally accusatory tone much less confrontational.

"I did," Dex said, but Aidan could see his eyes flash in annoyance. Like Dexter would ever forget the tools. Aidan rolled his eyes because he knew his boyfriend was too nice to ever do it.

Or maybe it was that Dex and Edmund had somehow, impossibly, become friends, and Dex didn't want to tell him he was being stupid in front of the huge contingent of elves, gathered to see them off.

"Good, because you never know when Santa will get a harebrained idea into his head that he needs to play matchmaker and ruin all our hard work, deliberately sabotaging the sleigh." Edmund kept a straight face almost the whole way through, but towards the end his smile, the one that Aidan hadn't been quite sure existed when he'd first moved here from Tír na nÓg, began to emerge.

Belinda had been wonderful for Edmund; making him understand that there was more to life than work.

But the real turning point for Edmund had been the arrival of Dexter at the North Pole. When Dexter had moved here, he'd wanted to know how everything worked. How he could make it work better.

He and Edmund had, to Aidan's complete disbelief, discovered a mutual admiration for each other, and they actually worked *together* now.

Dexter also worked for George, and liked to call himself George's apprentice, though George liked to grumble about his choice of words.

"You're no one's apprentice, boy, you're an accomplished engineer in your own right," George always said.

But Dex still did it, because Aidan knew he liked it.

"I did what was necessary," Sam said, raising his hands in mock surrender. But he was smiling, brightly. Shining, almost, the way he always did on Christmas, but this year, there was an extra shimmer to him.

Aidan and Dex had visited the pond yesterday, and had kissed under its watchful eye, celebrating how bright it had grown over the last six months. They were slowly beginning to mingle their two worlds.

The first step had been for Aidan to come to Chicago and to meet Jonathan.

Jonathan had been understandably confused. "I thought you'd said," he'd asked slowly, enunciating each word, "that you were going away for a very long time to work on a super secret government project."

"I did," Dex had said with a sheepish shrug. "But then Aidan had wanted to meet you."

It had been clear from the beginning that Aidan wasn't some secret government agent. Jonathan had figured out some of it, and then Dexter had told him the rest, with Aidan interjecting.

At first he hadn't believed, but they were going to bring him up to the North Pole for the next summer solstice, and it was mighty hard not to believe when Santa was right in front of you.

That was what Aidan was counting on.

Belief.

Neither it nor change was easy, but slowly but surely Aidan knew what he and Dex were doing was making a difference. And despite what Sam had said about Dexter not being necessary, Aidan had discovered that he was irreplaceable. He supported Aidan, loving him unconditionally, and it was always easier to butt heads with a difficult group of elves when he knew he'd be coming home to the man he loved, but it was more than that.

Dex brought change just by being who he was.

It was much tougher for elves to be afraid of him, once they got to know him. And Dexter was everywhere, always helping, always willing to lend a hand, always smiling. Everyone who met him loved him.

Aidan just loved him a little bit more.

"Are we ready to go?" Aidan asked.

He was ready, and even excited, to start the journey this year.

Over the last year, with Sam's help, and with Dex's, he'd found the role of Christmas Savior, and now Santa's right-hand elf, no longer felt too heavy and too difficult to bear.

He'd grown, and he'd learned to actually look forward to and enjoy all the cheer and joy that the elves spent the year spreading.

"I'm ready," Dexter said. "Tools and all."

Edmund was the one who actually rolled his eyes at that.

"Then go we shall," Sam announced, climbing into the sleigh and raising his arms, a cheer going up from the assembled elves.

"Come on, you two lovers, we've got presents to deliver and belief to bolster."

Dex got in first and offered a hand to Aidan, helping him into the sleigh.

When Dexter had initially suggested, a few months back, that he accompany Sam and Aidan on the annual Christmas Eve trip, Edmund had balked and gone totally silent, refusing to talk to Dex for days on end.

Everyone had tried to talk to him, but he'd refused to budge and refused to listen to reason.

It wasn't until Aidan went to see him, and laid out why exactly it was so important to incorporate some of the human world into their traditions, showing him the magic pool deep in the forest, that Edmund had finally relented.

"But I don't like it," Edmund had claimed at first.

But by Christmas Eve, even Edmund had completely come around to the idea. "It just makes sense," he'd said during the last staff meeting before the night itself, "to have the person *on* the sleigh who helped make all the new improvements to the sleigh."

So Aidan wouldn't be alone this year, with Sam. Dexter would be by his side, and he'd be lying if he said that wasn't partly why Aidan was looking forward to this so much.

Spending time with Dexter was something he'd never take for granted. His love was the most precious gift he'd ever received.

"Ready?" Sam asked them, flipping some switches.

"Let's see what this puppy can do," Dex said, sounding equally excited himself.

It might be for the sleigh, but then he reached down and took Aidan's hand in his own, squeezing it gently.

"I love you," Aidan murmured softly.

"Hold on," Sam called out, and the sleigh lifted off, the engine firing perfectly, and he zipped up and around the village, leaving a trail of glowing magical particles.

Aidan didn't know whether the swooping feeling in his stomach was the sudden sensation in the air, or if it was the tender, loving expression in Dex's dark eyes.

He'd refused to wear one of the traditional capes, so Belinda had fashioned him a bright red coat lined with fur, and Aidan thought it made him look even more impossibly handsome than the very first time he'd ever seen him.

"I love you, too," Dexter whispered back. "And I've got a gift for you, to prove just how much."

He whipped something out of one of the many pockets of his jacket, which he'd specifically requested that Belinda add.

"What's that?" Aidan asked, then Dex dangled it over their heads. "Is that . . . no, that isn't . . ."

"It's mistletoe," Dex said. "So you'd better kiss me now, elf of mine."

"You holding on?" Sam said as the sleigh shimmied. "This has got a lot of power, Dex. Good job."

"I enjoyed doing it, and yeah, we're good."

"Never better," Aidan agreed, and leaned in, pressing a warm kiss against Dex's mouth.

The sleigh turned abruptly, and jerked them apart.

"None of that mistletoe nonsense back there," Sam teased. "You two have your work cut out for you tonight. After all, it's Christmas!"

Aidan smiled at Dex.

"Merry Christmas, Dex," he said, "thanks for getting me everything I ever wanted. You're *almost* my favorite gift ever."

Dex smiled. "What's your favorite gift?" he asked, even though Aidan was pretty sure he knew.

"Milk and cookies."

It was a gift to watch Dex's face, his expressive dark eyes, and the love in them.

"It was absolutely my pleasure," Dex said, squeezing his hand, and truer words had never been spoken.

Make sure you sign up for my newsletter to never miss another Beth Bolden book.

You can sign up scanning the QR code below, or clicking the link above.

BETH'S BOOKS

FOOD TRUCK WARRIORS

Drive Me Crazy - Lucas is just looking for some summer fun while Tony wants it all. But when their undeniable chemistry heats up the food truck kitchen, all bets are off.

Kiss & Tell - a New Year's Eve novella set in the Food Truck Warriors universe. Jackson lives to work, but what happens when he runs into Greek food truck owner, Alexis? When midnight strikes, sparks fly, and two lives change forever.

Hit the Brakes - Tate has had a crush on famous football player Chase since high school. But what happens when Chase suggests they fake a relationship to give Tate's food truck a much-needed boost?

On a Roll - Sean and Gabriel accidentally named their food truck the exact same thing. Can they stop arguing about it long enough to fall in love?

Full Speed Ahead - Lennox isn't the only one keeping secrets.

A stalker has discovered one about Ash, and when Lennox intervenes, the electric chemistry between him and Ash erupts into something very much like love.

Wheels Down - Shaw isn't Ross' friend—Ross isn't sure he has friends, anyway—until he discovers that Shaw is actually so much more than just his friend. He's his lover, and his partner, and his salvation.

Ride or Die - Ren & Seth's story and the final Food Truck Warriors novel. Out January 2022.

KITCHEN GODS - Available on audio

Complete Box Set - including all four novels, and additional bonus content.

Bite Me - Miles' and Evan's story. They were sure they were enemies . . . until they were sure they weren't.

Catch Me - Wyatt and Ryan's story. Their relationship is completely fake . . . until it isn't.

Worship Me - a short story about Matt and Alex from Catch Me.

Savor Me - Xander and Damon's story. They're partners in a new restaurant . . . until they're so much more.

Indulge Me - Kian and Bastian's story. Working together is a necessity, but their mutual love? It's every bit an unnecessary indulgence.

LOS ANGELES RIPTIDE

The Rivalry - Rival. Enemy. Teammate. Friend. Lover. Two very different quarterbacks end up playing for the same team, fighting for the same starting spot - and end up fighting for each other, too. *Available on audio.*

Rough Contact - Their romance is forbidden. Their love is a secret. Neal and Jamie are the Romeo and Juliet of football - with all the feels, and much less tragedy.

The Red Zone - With Alec's help, Spencer can change everything about his life he's come to hate. An extraordinary future—and an undeniably extraordinary man—are waiting for him.

STAR SHADOW

Complete Box Set - including all four novels, and an exclusive short story.

Terrible Things - a little grittier, a little darker, a little more terrible. A rock star romance. Available on audio.

Impossible Things - Benji & Diego's story, and the sequel to Terrible Things. Available on audio.

Hazardous Things - Felix's had a crush on Max forever. But he's straight. Ish. Right?

Extraordinary Things - The final book of the Star Shadow series. Revisits Leo & Caleb's love story.

STANDALONES

Merry Elf-ing Christmas - a North Pole elf who doesn't belong, and an engineer who doesn't realize what he's missing in his life is Christmas magic. Coming November 18.

The Rainbow Clause - Shy NFL quarterback meets immovable object AKA the journalist assigned to write his coming out profile. Sparks are definitely gonna fly. Available on audio.

All Screwed Up - David is Griffin's annoying contractor. So why does Griffin want David to nail him? An enemies to lovers romantic comedy co-authored with Brittany Cournoyer.

Snow Job - Micah & Jake have always been enemies. They used to be stepbrothers. But they could be so much more.

Taste on my Tongue - Kitchen Wars is the hottest new reality show on TV, but pop star Landon can't even turn an oven on. Will baker Quentin be able to give him a culinary education so they can win?

Wrapped with Love - Losing Jordan is the biggest regret of Reed's life. Will Secret Santa and a little holiday magic be able to repair what was broken?

Fairytale of LaGuardia - Once upon a holiday season, a hockey player and a baseball player walked into a bar . . .and the rest is history. A Christmas story co-authored with A.E. Wasp.

Musical Notes - Two teachers with nothing in common, except a high school musical that's only three weeks away from Opening Night.

FANTASY

Yours, Forever After - a lost Prince, a lonely bookworm and a surprisingly chatty unicorn go on the quest of a lifetime to save their kingdoms from an evil sorceress. Now available in the Complete Edition, featuring an epilogue novella. Available on audio.

About Beth

A lifelong Pacific Northwester, **Beth Bolden** has just recently moved to North Carolina with her supportive husband. Beth still believes in Keeping Portland Weird, and intends to be just as weird in Raleigh.

Beth has been writing practically since she learned the alphabet. Unfortunately, her first foray into novel writing, titled *Big Bear with Sparkly Earrings*, wasn't a bestseller, but hope springs eternal. She's published twenty-eight novels and seven novellas.

Join Beth's Boldest, her Reader's Group
Subscribe to Beth's Newsletter
Follow Beth on BookBub
Facebook / Instagram / Twitter
www.bethbolden.com